OTHER BOOKS BY TIM POWERS

Praise for Tim Powers

"These smart, always-engaging stories, so open to mystery and speculation, demonstrate once again that Tim Powers rocks, rules, and prevails. He is one of the best, most significant writers in this country, and 'A Time to Cast Away Stones' is one of his masterpieces."

—Peter Straub,
author of *Ghost Story* and *A Dark Matter*

"One of the most original and innovative writers... the quality of Powers' prose never falters.... His writing defies characterization and he never repeats himself."

—*Washington Post Book World*

"Whether writing about zombie pirates of the Caribbean (*On Stranger Tides*), female vampires preying on Romantic poets (*The Stress of Her Regard*), or the escapades of a time traveler in 19th-century England (*The Anubis Gates*), Powers always goes the distance, never taking easy shortcuts that tempt authors with lesser imaginations."

—*San Francisco Chronicle*

"Tim Powers is a brilliant writer."

—William Gibson,
author of *Neuromancer* and *Spook Country*

"Powers orchestrates reality and fantasy so artfully that the reader is not allowed a moment's doubt."

—*The New Yorker*

"The reigning king of adult historical fantasy…"

−*Kirkus*

"Powers plots like a demon."

−*Village Voice*

"…a reigning master of adult contemporary fantasy."

−*Booklist*

"Philip K. Dick felt that one day Tim Powers would be one of our greatest fantasy writers. Phil was right."

−Roger Zelazny,
author of *Nine Princes in Amber* and *Lord of Light*

"Powers has already proved that he is a master of what he terms 'doing card tricks in the dark,' referring to the incredible amount of historical, biographical, and practical research that goes into his works."

−*Harvard Review*

"The best fantasy writer to appear in decades."

−*Manchester Guardian*

"Tim Powers is a genius."

−Algis Budrys

"…one of fantasy's major stylists…"

−*SF Site*

THE BIBLE REPAIRMAN

AND OTHER STORIES

•••

Tim Powers

TACHYON PUBLICATIONS • SAN FRANCISCO

The Bible Repairman and Other Stories
© 2011 by Tim Powers

• • •

Cover design by Josh Beatman
Interior design by Jacob McMurray

TACHYON PUBLICATIONS
1459 18th Street #139
San Francisco, CA 94107
(415) 285-5615
tachyon@tachyonpublications.com

SMART SCIENCE FICTION & FANTASY
www.tachyonpublications.com

Series Editor: Jacob Weisman
Project Editor: Jill Roberts

ISBN 13: 978-1-61696-047-6
ISBN 10: 1-61696-047-7

First Edition: 2011
Printed in the United States of America by Worzalla
9 8 7 6 5 4 3 2 1

TABLE OF CONTENTS

• • •

To Karen Purvis,
for advice and friendship

INTRODUCTION

•••

When people ask me what it was that I was trying to say, in this-or-that story, I like to answer with a line from an old Dave Barry article: "Nobody wins when you play games with traffic safety." Or, "Floss your teeth for better dental hygiene."

The thing is – as far as I can recall – I've never tried to make a point in any of my stories, never "had something to say." Writers like C. S. Lewis or George Orwell can do that and somehow make a compelling story too, but if I tried it I'm sure I'd wind up with a tiresome quasi-allegory.

Of course some "theme" or other is present in just about any story, even when the theme isn't inserted deliberately. (In fact deliberate themes can turn out to be in conflict with the themes the subconscious sneaks in, which makes for a jarring story!) I've sometimes reread an old book of mine and found at least rudimentary themes working – one of my books seemed to have "something to say" about the value of children, for example, though at least consciously I'm indifferent to children. And I've noticed a lot of fathers-and-sons conflicts in my books, though in fact I always got along fine with my own father.

But I'm happy to leave my fictional themes, such as they may be, to sort themselves out.

And there are plot elements, too, that seem to show up repeatedly of their own accord. One time somebody pointed out to me that most of my books ended with the protagonist going away in a boat; I checked it out, and sure enough, he was right. I was mildly pleased with this insistent element from my subconscious, but at the same time I realized that I would now have to stop it – if I were to do it again in the next book, it would at that point be just a forced gesture, an arbitrary consistency. So I made a resolution – no more boats at the end!

Later it occurred to me to go back and see what I had done instead; and I found that the next book I had written ended with a woman beckoning to my protagonist from the far side of a pond…and then, instead of walking around the shoreline, he walks straight across to her, wading right through the pond.

Interesting! But of course after noticing that, I couldn't end a book with any sort of travel-across-water at all.

I hope nobody points out to me any more accidentally recurrent elements in my books!

But there are things I do deliberately.

●●

One day in late '81 or early '82, I drove Philip K. Dick to his doctor because Phil had decided that he had a hernia. I read a book in the waiting room while the doctor looked him over, and eventually Phil came out.

He was looking crestfallen, and as we left he explained that – it turned out – he didn't have a hernia after all. He brooded about it on the drive home.

"You know, Powers," he said eventually, "I'm always going to the doctor with a diagnosis all figured out, but I've always got it wrong. The doctor must think I'm nuts. When I walk in, he always just...sighs, and asks me what it is *now* that I think I've got." Phil shook his head. "And then I'm lucky if there's anything wrong with me at all."

• •

And one day when I was a teenager watching television, our Saint Bernard came blundering into the living room, having noticed, apparently for the first time, the TV's voices and moving images. The dog sniffed at the screen, hurried around to the back of the set and sniffed there, pondered it all for a few seconds, and finally nodded and walked away.

• •

Phil, and probably the dog too, were wrong in the conclusions they came to, but they both believed they had *figured something out*. Phil learned better – as he so often did – but the dog probably believed for the rest of his life that he had figured out the television.

In my stories I try to have plots – I try to set up apparently disconnected events and then make sense of them. Figure them out! I want my readers to be satisfied, like the St. Bernard, and not be left with an anticlimax, as Phil was.

Of course we can safely assume that the St. Bernard was wrong in whatever conclusion he came to, and of course Phil was fortunate that his conclusion was a mistake. Still, certainty is reassuring.

In the stories I most like to read, things eventually prove to make sense. The events might be outlandish, and the resolution might be as objectively impossible as a dog's explanation of television, but it's all presented sincerely, not ironically, not tongue-in-cheek. Loose ends are tied up. The writer has taken the characters and their concerns seriously, so I can too, and has shown how all the conflicts and oxymorons are reconciled.

Real life, of course, doesn't provide this. Edward John Trelawny, whom I used as a character in my story "A Time to Cast Away Stones," was a real historical person who compensated for the pointless shabbiness of his actual life by inventing a glamorous biography for himself, and eventually he even came to believe that well-plotted fiction himself.

I sympathize. Real life is generally very haphazard in its plotting, and I think a lot of people lament that, and turn to fiction to briefly experience, albeit vicariously, a more satisfying sort of reality. We want to see *sense* — not necessarily happy endings, but effectual actions and significant outcomes. (Postmodern fiction and metafiction, I gather, aim to call attention to the falsity of these things, which is like selling liquor that perversely makes you more sober.)

Our inclination to look for sense in the world doesn't, of course, prove that there's any out there to be found. Being hungry doesn't prove we have bread, as Matthew Arnold is supposed to have written.

But, as C. S. Lewis points out, being hungry does imply the existence of bread.

So I'm on the side of Phil Dick and the dog.

The Bible Repairman

and Other Stories

THE BIBLE REPAIRMAN

●●●

"It'll do to kiss the book on still, won't it?" growled Dick,
who was evidently uneasy at the curse he had brought on
himself.

"A Bible with a bit cut out!" returned Silver derisively. "Not
it. It don't bind no more'n a ballad-book."

"Don't it, though?" cried Dick, with a sort of joy. "Well I
reckon that's worth having, too."

— Treasure Island,
Robert Louis Stevenson

Across the highway was old Humberto, a dark spot against the tan field
between the railroad tracks and the freeway fence, pushing a stripped-
down shopping cart along the cracked sidewalk. His shadow still
stretched halfway to the center-divider line in the early morning sunlight, but he was apparently already very drunk, and he was using the
shopping cart as a walker, bracing his weight on it as he shuffled along.
Probably he never slept at all, not that he was ever really awake either.

Humberto had done a lot of work in his time, and the people he talked
and gestured to were, at best, long gone and probably existed now only

in his cannibalized memory – but this morning as Torrez watched him the old man clearly looked across the street straight at Torrez and waved. He was just a silhouette against the bright eastern daylight – his camouflage pants, white beard and Daniel Boone coonskin cap were all one raggedly backlit outline – but he might have been smiling too.

After a moment's hesitation Torrez waved and nodded. Torrez was not drunk in the morning, nor unable to walk without leaning on something, nor surrounded by imaginary acquaintances, and he meant to sustain those differences between them – but he supposed that he and Humberto were brothers in the trades, and he should show some respect to a player who simply had not known when to retire.

Torrez pocketed his Camels and his change and turned his back on the old man, and trudged across the parking lot toward the path that led across a weedy field to home.

He was retired, at least from the big-stakes dives. Nowadays he just waded a little ways out – he worked on cars and Bibles and second-hand eyeglasses and clothes people bought at thrift stores, and half of that work was just convincing the customers that work had been done. He always had to use holy water – *real* holy water, from gallon jugs he filled from the silver urn at St. Anne's – but though it impressed the customers, all he could see that it actually did was get stuff wet. Still, it was better to err on the side of thoroughness.

His garage door was open, and several goats stood up with their hoofs on the fence rail of the lot next door. Torrez paused to pull up some of the tall, furry, sage-like weeds that sprang up in every stretch of unattended dirt in the county, and he held them out and let the goats chew them up. Sometimes when customers arrived at times like this, Torrez would whisper to the goats and then pause and nod.

Torrez's Toyota stood at the curb because a white Dodge Dart was parked in the driveway. Torrez had already installed a "pain button" on the Dodge's dashboard, so that when the car wouldn't start, the owner could give the car a couple of jabs — *Oh yeah? How do you like this, eh?* On the other side of the firewall the button was connected to a wire that was screwed to the carburetor housing; nonsense, but the stuff had to look convincing.

Torrez had also used a can of Staples compressed air and a couple of magnets to try to draw a babbling ghost out of the car's stereo system, and this had not been nonsense — if he had properly opposed the magnets to the magnets in the speakers, and got the Bernoulli effect with the compressed air sprayed over the speaker diaphragm, then at speeds over forty there would no longer be a droning imbecile monologue faintly going on behind whatever music was playing. Torrez would take the Dodge out onto the freeway today, assuming the old car would get up to freeway speeds, and try it out driving north, east, south and west. Two hundred dollars if the voice was gone, and a hundred in any case for the pain button.

And he had a couple of Bibles in need of customized repair, and those were an easy fifty dollars apiece — just brace the page against a piece of plywood in a frame and scorch out the verses the customers found intolerable, with a wood-burning stylus; a plain old razor wouldn't have the authority that hot iron did. And then of course drench the defaced book in holy water to validate the edited text. Matthew 19:5-6 and Mark 10:7-12 were bits he was often asked to burn out, since they condemned re-marriage after divorce, but he also got a lot of requests to lose Matthew 25:41 through 46, with Jesus's promise of Hell to stingy people. And he offered a special deal to eradicate all thirty or so mentions of adultery. Some of these customized Bibles ended up after a few years with hardly any weight besides the binding.

He pushed open the front door of the house – he never locked it – and made his way to the kitchen to get a beer out of the cold spot in the sink. The light was blinking on the telephone answering machine, and when he had popped the can of Budweiser he pushed the play button.

"Give Mr. Torrez this message," said a recorded voice. "Write down the number I give you! It is important, make sure he gets it!" The voice recited a number then, and Torrez wrote it down. His answering machine had come with a pre-recorded message on it in a woman's voice – *No one is available to take your call right now* – and many callers assumed the voice was that of a woman he was living with. Apparently she sounded unreliable, for they often insisted several times that she convey their messages to him.

He punched in the number, and a few moments later a man at the other end of the line was saying to him, "Mr. Torrez? We need your help, like you helped out the Fotas four years ago. Our daughter was stolen, and now we've got a ransom note – she was in a coffee pot with roses tied around it –"

"I don't do that work anymore," Torrez interrupted, "I'm sorry. Mr. Seaweed in Corona still does – he's younger – I could give you his number."

"I called him already a week ago, but then I heard you were back in business. You're better than Seaweed –"

Poor old Humberto had kept on doing deep dives. Torrez had done them longer than he should have, and nowadays couldn't understand a lot of the books he had loved when he'd been younger.

"I'm not back in that business," he said. "I'm very sorry." He hung up the phone.

He had not even done the ransom negotiations when it had been his own daughter that had been stolen, three years ago – and his wife had left him over it, not understanding that she would probably have had to

4

be changing her mentally retarded husband's diapers forever afterward if he had done it.

Torrez's daughter Amelia had died at the age of eight, of a fever. Her grave was in the dirt lot behind the Catholic cemetery, and on most Sundays Torrez and his wife had visited the grave and made sure there were lots of little stuffed animals and silver foil pinwheels arranged on the dirt, and for a marker they had set into the ground a black plastic box with a clear top, with her death-certificate displayed in it to show that she had died in a hospital. And her soul had surely gone to Heaven, but they had caught her ghost to keep it from wandering in the noisy, cold half-world, and Torrez had bound it into one of Amelia's cloth dolls. Every Sunday night they had put candy and cigarettes and a shot-glass of rum in front of the doll – hardly appropriate fare for a little girl, but ghosts were somehow all the same age. Torrez had always lit the cigarettes and stubbed them out before laying them in front of the doll, and bitten the candies: ghosts needed somebody to have *started* such things for them.

And then one day the house had been broken into, and the little shrine and the doll were gone, replaced with a ransom note: *If you want your daughter's ghost back, Mr. Torrez, give me some of your blood.* And there had been a phone number.

Usually these ransom notes asked the recipient to get a specific tattoo that corresponded to a tattoo on the kidnapper's body – and afterward whichever family member complied would have lost a lot of memories, and be unable to feel affection, and never again dream at night. The kidnapper would have taken those things. But a kidnapper would always settle instead for the blood of a person whose soul was broken in the way that Torrez's was, and so the robbed families would often come to Torrez and offer him a lot of money to step in and give up some of his blood, and save them the fearful obligation of the vampiric tattoo.

Sometimes the kidnapper was the divorced father or mother of the ghost – courts never considered custody of a dead child – or a suitor who had been rejected long before, and in these cases there would be no ransom demand; but then it had sometimes been possible for Torrez to trace the thief and steal the ghost back, in whatever pot or box or liquor bottle it had been confined in.

But in most cases he had had to go through with the deal, meet the kidnapper somewhere and give up a cupful or so of blood to retrieve the stolen ghost; and each time, along with the blood, he had lost a piece of his soul.

The phone began ringing again as Torrez tipped up the can for the last sip of beer; he ignored it.

Ten years ago it had been an abstract consideration – when he had thought about it at all, he had supposed that he could lose a lot of his soul without missing it, and he'd told himself that his soul was bound for Hell anyway, since he had deliberately broken it when he was eighteen, and so dispersing it had just seemed like hiding money from the IRS. But by the time he was thirty-five his hair had gone white and he had lost most of the sight in his left eye because of ruptured blood-vessels behind the retina, and he could no longer understand the plots of long novels he tried to read. Apparently some sort of physical and mental integrity was lost too, along with the blood and the bits of his hypothetical soul.

But what the kidnappers wanted from Torrez's blood was not vicarious integrity – it was nearly the opposite. Torrez thought of it as spiritual botox.

The men and women who stole ghosts for ransom were generally mediums, fortune-tellers, psychics – always clairvoyant. And even more than the escape that could be got from extorted dreams and memories and the ability to feel affection, they needed to be able to selectively blunt the psychic noise of humans living and dead.

Torrez imagined it as a hundred radios going at once all the time, and half the announcers moronically drunk – crying, giggling, trying to start fights.

He would never know. He had broken all the antennae in his own soul when he was eighteen, by killing a man who attacked him with a knife in a parking lot one midnight. Torrez had wrestled the knife away from the drunken assailant and had knocked the man unconscious by slamming his head into the bumper of a car – but then Torrez had picked up the man's knife and, just because he could, had driven it into the unconscious man's chest. The District Attorney had eventually called it self-defense, a justifiable homicide, and no charges were brought against Torrez, but his soul was broken.

The answering machine clicked on, but only the dial tone followed the recorded message. Torrez dropped the Budweiser can into the trash basket and walked into the living room, which over the years had become his workshop.

Murder seemed to be the crime that broke souls most effectively, and Torrez had done his first ghost-ransom job for free that same year, in 1983, just to see if his soul was now a source of the temporary disconnection-from-humanity that the psychics valued so highly. And he had tested out fine.

He had been doing Bible repair for twenty years, but his reputation in that cottage industry had been made only a couple of years ago, by accident. Three Jehovah's Witnesses had come to his door one summer day, wearing suits and ties, and he had stepped outside to debate scripture with them. "Let me see your Bible," he had said, "and I'll show you right in there why you're wrong," and when they handed him the book he had flipped to the first chapter of John's gospel and started reading. This was after his vision had begun to go bad, though, and he'd had to read it with a magnifying glass, and it had been a sunny day – and he had inadvertently set their Bible on fire. They had left hurriedly, and apparently told everyone in the neighborhood that Torrez could burn a Bible just by touching it.

●●

He was bracing a tattered old Bible in the frame on the marble-topped table, ready to scorch out St. Paul's adverse remarks about homosexuality for a customer, when he heard three knocks at his front door, the first one loud and the next two just glancing scuffs, and he realized he had not closed the door and the knocks had pushed it open. He made sure his woodburning stylus was lying in the ashtray, then hurried to the entry hall.

Framed in the bright doorway was a short stocky man with a moustache, holding a shoebox and shifting from one foot to the other.

"Mr. Torrez," the man said. He smiled, and a moment later looked as if he'd never smile again. He waved the shoebox toward Torrez and said, "A man has stolen my daughter."

Perhaps the shoebox was the shrine he had kept his daughter's ghost in, in some jelly jar or perfume bottle. Probably there were ribbons and candy hearts around the empty space where the daughter's ghost-container had lain. Still, a shoebox was a pretty nondescript shrine; but maybe it was just for travelling, like a cat-carrier box.

"I just called," the man said, "and got your woman. I hoped she was wrong, and you were here."

"I don't do that work anymore," said Torrez patiently, "ransoming ghosts. You want to call Seaweed in Corona."

"I don't want you to ransom a ghost," the man said, holding the box toward Torrez. "I already had old Humberto do that, yesterday. This is for you."

"If Humberto ransomed your daughter," Torrez said carefully, nodding toward the box but not taking it, "then why are you here?"

"*My* daughter is *not* a ghost. My daughter is twelve years old, and this man took her when she was walking home from school. I can pay you fifteen hundred dollars to get her back – this is extra, a gift for you, from me, with the help of Humberto."

Torrez had stepped back. "Your daughter was kidnapped? Alive? Good God, man, call the police right now! The FBI! You don't come to *me* with –"

"The police would not take the ransom note seriously," the man said, shaking his head. "They would think he wants money really, they would not think of his terms being sincerely meant, as he wrote them!" He took a deep breath and let it out. "Here," he said, extending the box again.

Torrez took the box – it was light – and cautiously lifted the lid.

Inside, in a nest of rosemary sprigs and Catholic holy cards, lay a little cloth doll that Torrez recognized.

"Amelia," he said softly.

He lifted it out of the box, and he could feel the quiver of his own daughter's long-lost ghost in it.

"Humberto bought this back for you?" Torrez asked. Three years after her kidnapping, he thought. No wonder Humberto waved to me this morning! I hope he didn't have to spend much of his soul on her; he's got no more than a mouse's worth left.

"For you," the man said. "She is a gift. Save my daughter."

Torrez didn't want to invite the man into the house. "What did the ransom note for your daughter say?"

"It said, Juan-Manuel Ortega – that's me – I have Elizabeth, and I will kill her and take all her blood unless you *induce* Terry Torrez to come to me and him give me the ransom blood instead."

"Call the police," Torrez said. "That's a bluff, about taking her blood. Why would he want a little girl's blood? When did this happen? Every minute –"

Juan-Manuel Ortega opened his mouth very wide, as if to pronounce some big syllable, then closed it. "My Elizabeth," he said, "she – killed her sister last year. My rifle was in the closet – she didn't know, she's a child, she didn't know it was loaded –"

Torrez could feel that his eyebrows were raised. Yes she did, he thought; she killed her sister deliberately, and broke her own soul doing it, and the kidnapper knows it even if you truly don't.

Your daughter's a murderer. She's like me.

Still, her blood – her broken, blunting soul – wouldn't be accessible to the kidnapper, the way Torrez's would be, unless…

"Has your daughter –" He had spoken too harshly, and tried again. "Has she ever used magic?" Or is her soul still virginal, he thought.

Ortega bared his teeth and shrugged. "Maybe! She said she caught her sister's ghost in my electric shaver. I – I think she did. I don't use it anymore, but think I hear it in the nights."

Then her blood will do for the kidnapper what mine would, Torrez thought. Not quite as well, since my soul is surely more opaque – older and more stained by the use of magic – but hers will do if he can't get mine.

"Here is my phone number," said Ortega, now shoving a business card at Torrez and talking too rapidly to interrupt, "and the kidnapper has your number. He wants only you. I am leaving it in your hands. Save my daughter, please."

Then he turned around and ran down the walkway to a van parked behind Torrez's Toyota. Torrez started after him, but the sun-glare in his bad left eye made him uncertain of his footing, and he stopped when he heard the van shift into gear and start away. The man's wife must have been waiting behind the wheel.

I should call the police myself, Torrez thought as he lost sight of the van in the brightness. But he's right, the police would take the kidnapping seriously, but not the ransom. The kidnapper doesn't want money – he wants my blood, me.

A living girl! he thought. I don't save living people, I save ghosts. And I don't even do that anymore.

She's like me.

He shuffled back into the house, and set the cloth doll on the kitchen counter, sitting up against the toaster. Almost without thinking about it, he took the pack of Camels out of his shirt pocket and lit one with his Bic lighter, then stubbed it out on the stovetop and laid it on the tile beside the doll.

The tip of the cigarette glowed again, and the telephone rang. He just kept staring at the doll and the smoldering cigarette and let the phone ring.

The answering machine clicked in, and he heard the woman's recorded voice say, "No one is available to take your call, he had me on his TV, Daddy, so I could change channels for him. 'Two, four, eleven,' and I'd change them."

Torrez became aware that he had sat down on the linoleum floor. Her ghost had never found a way to speak when he and his ex-wife had had possession of it. "I'm sorry, Amelia," he said hoarsely. "It would have killed me to buy you back. They don't want money, they –"

"What?" said the voice of the caller. "Is Mr. Torrez there?"

"Rum he gave me, at least," said Amelia's voice. "It wouldn't have killed you, not really."

Torrez got to his feet, feeling much older than his actual forty years. He opened the high cupboard and saw her bottle of 151-proof rum still standing up there beside the stacked china dishes he never used. He hoisted the bottle down and wiped dust off it.

"I'm going to tell him how rude you are," said the voice on the phone, "this isn't very funny." The line clicked.

"No," Torrez said as he poured a couple of ounces of rum into a coffee cup. "It wouldn't have killed me. But it would have made a mindless... it would have made an idiot of me. I wouldn't have been able to...work, talk, think." Even now I can hardly make sense of the comics in the newspaper, he thought.

"He had me on his TV, Daddy," said Amelia's voice from the answering machine. "I was his channel-changer."

Torrez set the coffee cup near the doll, and felt it vibrate faintly just as he let go of the handle. The sharp alcohol smell became stronger, as if some of the rum had been vaporized.

"And he gave me candy."

"I'm sorry," said Torrez absently, "I don't have any candy."

"Sugar Babies are better than Reese's Pieces." Torrez had always given her Reese's Pieces, but before now she had not been able to tell him what she preferred.

"How can you talk?"

"The people that nobody paid for, he would put all of us, all our jars and boxes and dolls on the TV and make us change what the TV people said. We made them say bad prayers."

The phone rang again, and Amelia's voice out of the answering machine speaker said, "Sheesh" and broke right in. "What, what?"

"I've got a message for Terry Torrez," said a woman's voice, "make sure he gets it, write this number down!" The woman recited a number, which Torrez automatically memorized. "My husband is in an alarm clock, but he's fading; I don't hardly dream about him even with the clock under the pillow anymore, and the mint patties, it's like a year he takes to even get halfway through one! He needs a booster shot, tell Terry Torrez that, and I'll pay a thousand dollars for it."

I'll want more than a thousand, Torrez thought, and she'll pay more, too. Booster shot! The only way to boost a fading ghost – and they all faded sooner or later – was to add to the container a second ghost, the ghost of a newly deceased infant, which would have vitality but no personality to interfere with the original ghost.

Torrez had done that a few times, and – though these were only ghosts, not souls, not actual people! – it had always felt like putting feeder mice into an aquarium with an old, blind snake.

"That'll buy a lot of Sugar Babies," remarked Amelia's ghost.

"What? Just make sure he gets the message!"

The phone clicked off, and Amelia said, "I remember the number."

"So do I."

Midwives sold newborn ghosts. The thought of looking one of them up nauseated him.

"Mom's dead," said Amelia.

Torrez opened his mouth, then just exhaled. He took a sip of Amelia's rum and said, "She is?"

"Sure. We all know, when someone is. I guess they figured you wouldn't bleed for her, if you wouldn't bleed for me. Sugar Babies are better than Reese's Pieces."

"Right, you said."

"Can I have her rings? They'd fit on my head like crowns."

"I don't know what became of her," he said. It's true, he realized, I don't. I don't even know what there was of her.

He looked at the doll and wondered why anyone kept such things.

His own Bible, on the mantel in the living room workshop, was relatively intact, though of course it was warped from having been soaked in holy water. He had burned out half a dozen verses from the Old Testament that had to do with witchcraft and wizards; and he had thought about excising "thou shalt not kill" from Exodus, but decided that if the commandment was gone, his career might be too.

After he had refused to ransom Amelia's ghost, he had cut out Ezekiel 44:25 – "And they shall come at no dead person to defile themselves: but for father, or for mother, or for son, or for daughter, for brother, or for sister that hath had no husband, they may defile themselves."

He had refused to defile himself – defile himself any further, at least – for his own dead daughter. And so she had wound up helping to voice "bad prayers" out of a TV set somewhere.

The phone rang again, and this time he snatched up the receiver before the answering machine could come on. "Yes?"

"Mr. Torrez," said a man's voice. "I have a beaker of silence here, she's twelve years old and she's not in any jar or bottle."

"Her father has been here," Torrez said.

"I'd rather have the beaker that's you. For all her virtues, her soul's a bit thin still, and noises would get through."

Torrez remembered stories he'd heard about clairvoyants driven to insanity by the constant din of thoughts.

"My daddy doesn't play that anymore," said Amelia. "He has me back now."

Torrez remembered Humberto's wave this morning. Torrez had waved back.

Torrez looked into the living room, at the current Bible in the burning rack, and at the books he still kept on a shelf over the cold fireplace – paperbacks, hardcovers with gold-stamped titles, books in battered dust-jackets. He had found – what? – a connection with other people's lives, in them, which since the age of eighteen he had not been able to have in any other way. But these days their pages might as well all be blank. When he occasionally pulled one down and opened it, squinting through his magnifying glass to be able to see the print clearly, he could understand individual words but the sentences didn't cohere anymore.

She's like me.

I wonder if I could have found my way back, if I'd tried. I could tell her father to ask her to try.

"Bring the girl to where we meet," Torrez said. He leaned against the kitchen counter. In spite of his resolve, he was dizzy. "I'll have her parents with me to drive her away."

I'm dead already, he thought. Her father came to me, but the book says he may do that for a daughter. And for me, the dead person, this is the only way left to have a vital connection with other people's lives, even if they are strangers.

"And you'll come away with me," said the man's voice.

"No," said Amelia, "he won't. He brings me rum and candy."

The living girl who had been Amelia would have been at least somewhat concerned about the kidnapped girl. We each owe God our mind, Torrez thought, and he that gives it up today is paid off for tomorrow.

"Yes," said Torrez. He lifted the coffee cup; his hand was shaky, but he carefully poured the rum over the cloth head of the doll; the rum soaked into its fabric and puddled on the counter.

"How much is the ransom?" he asked.

"Only a reasonable amount," the voice assured him blandly.

Torrez was relieved; he was sure a reasonable amount was all that was left, and the kidnapper was likely to take it all anyway. He flicked his lighter over the doll, and then the doll was in a teardrop-shaped blue glare on the counter. Torrez stepped back, ready to wipe a wet towel over the cabinets if they should start to smolder. The doll turned black and began to come apart.

Amelia's voice didn't speak from the answering machine, though he thought he might have heard a long sigh – of release, he hoped.

"I want something," Torrez said. "A condition."

"What?"

"Do you have a Bible? Not a repaired one, a whole one?"

"I can get one."

"Yes, get one. And bring it for me."

"Okay. So we have a deal?"

The rum had burned out and the doll was a black pile, still glowing red here and there. He filled the cup with water from the tap and poured it over the ashes, and then there was no more red glow.

Torrez sighed, seeming to empty his lungs. "Yes. Where do we meet?"

●●●

I wrote this story after watching the movie Man on Fire, *caught up with the idea of a kidnap negotiator who finds that he has somehow got to the point where he must sacrifice himself in order to free the victim. And I used my local San Bernardino neighborhood as a setting, which led inevitably to the peculiarly pragmatic Hispanic style of magic.*

For the Subterranean Press limited edition I did several illustrations, and a reader at Amazon.com noted that I'm not a very good artist. Glancing at the limited edition, I was forced to agree. The reader of this book is fortunate that those illustrations haven't been reproduced here!

–T. P.

A Soul in a Bottle

•••

The forecourt of the Chinese Theater smelled of rain-wet stone and car exhaust, but a faint aroma like pears and cumin seemed to cling to his shirt-collar as he stepped around the clustered tourists, who all appeared to be blinking up at the copper towers above the forecourt wall or smiling into cameras as they knelt to press their hands into the puddled handprints in the cement paving blocks.

George Sydney gripped his shopping bag under his arm and dug three pennies from his pants pocket.

For the third or fourth time this morning he found himself glancing sharply over his left shoulder, but again there was no one within yards of him. The morning sun was bright on the Roosevelt Hotel across the boulevard, and the clouds were breaking up in the blue sky.

He crouched beside Jean Harlow's square and carefully laid one penny in each of the three round indentations below her incised signature, then wiped his wet fingers on his jacket. The coins wouldn't stay there long, but Sydney always put three fresh ones down whenever he walked past this block of Hollywood Boulevard.

He straightened up and again caught a whiff of pears and cumin, and when he glanced over his left shoulder there was a girl standing right behind him.

At first glance he thought she was a teenager – she was a head shorter than him, and her tangled red hair framed a narrow, freckled face with squinting eyes and a wide, amused mouth.

"*Three* pennies?" she asked, and her voice was deeper than he would have expected.

She was standing so close to him that his elbow had brushed her breasts when he'd turned around.

"That's right," said Sydney, stepping back from her, awkwardly so as not to scuff the coins loose.

"Why?"

"Uh…" He waved at the cement square and then barely caught his shopping bag. "People pried up the original three," he said. "For souvenirs. That she put there. Jean Harlow, when she put her handprints and shoe prints in the wet cement, in 1933."

The girl raised her faint eyebrows and blinked down at the stone. "I never knew that. How did you know that?"

"I looked her up one time. Uh, on Google."

The girl laughed quietly, and in that moment she seemed to be the only figure in the forecourt, including himself, that had color. He realized dizzily that the scent he'd been catching all morning was hers.

"Google?" she said. "Sounds like a Chinaman trying to say something. Are you always so nice to dead people?"

Her black linen jacket and skirt were visibly damp, as if she had slept outside, and seemed to be incongruously formal. He wondered if somebody had donated the suit to the Salvation Army place down the boulevard by Pep Boys, and if this girl was one of the young people he sometimes saw in sleeping bags under the marquee of a closed theater down there.

"Respectful, at least," he said, "I suppose."

She nodded. "'Lo,'" she said, "'some we loved, the loveliest and the best…'"

Surprised by the quote, he mentally recited the next two lines of the Rubaiyat quatrain – *That Time and Fate of all their Vintage prest, / Have drunk their cup a round or two before* – and found himself saying the last line out loud: "'And one by one crept silently to Rest.'"

She was looking at him intently, so he cleared his throat and said, "Are you local? You've been here before, I gather." Probably that odd scent was popular right now, he thought, the way patchouli oil had apparently been in the '6os. Probably he had brushed past someone who had been wearing it too, earlier in the day.

"I'm staying at the Heroic," she said, then went on quickly, "Do you live near here?"

He could see her bra through her damp white blouse, and he looked away – though he had noticed that it seemed to be embroidered with vines.

"I have an apartment up on Franklin," he said, belatedly.

She had noticed his glance, and arched her back for a moment before pulling her jacket closed and buttoning it. "'And in a Windingsheet of Vineleaf wrapped,'" she said merrily, "'So bury me by some sweet Gardenside.'"

Embarrassed, he muttered the first line of that quatrain: "'Ah, with the grape my fading life provide...'"

"Good idea!" she said – then she frowned, and her face was older. "No, dammit, I've got to go – but I'll see you again, right? I like you." She leaned forward and tipped her face up – and then she had briefly kissed him on the lips, and he did drop his shopping bag.

When he had crouched to pick it up and brushed the clinging drops of cold water off on his pants, and looked around, she was gone. He took a couple of steps toward the theater entrance, but the dozens of colorfully dressed strangers blocked his view, and he couldn't tell if she had hurried inside; and he didn't see her among the people by the photo booths or on the shiny black sidewalk.

Her lips had been hot – perhaps she had a fever.

He opened the plastic bag and peered inside, but the book didn't seem to have got wet or landed on a corner. A first edition of Colleen Moore's *Silent Star*, with a TLS, a typed letter, signed, tipped in on the front flyleaf. The Larry Edmunds Bookstore a few blocks east was going to give him fifty dollars for it.

And he thought he'd probably stop at Boardner's afterward and have a couple of beers before walking back to his apartment. Or maybe a shot of Wild Turkey, though it wasn't yet noon. He knew he'd be coming back here again, soon, frequently – peering around, lingering, almost certainly uselessly.

Still, *I'll see you again*, she had said. *I like you.*

Well, he thought with a nervous smile as he started east down the black sidewalk, stepping around the inset brass-rimmed pink stars with names on them, I like you too. Maybe, after all, it's a rain-damp street girl that I can fall in love with.

●●

She wasn't at the Chinese Theater when he looked for her there during the next several days, but a week later he saw her again. He was driving across Fairfax on Santa Monica Boulevard, and he saw her standing on the sidewalk in front of the big Starbuck's, in the shadows below the aquamarine openwork dome.

He knew it was her, though she was wearing jeans and a sweatshirt now – her red hair and freckled face were unmistakable. He honked the horn as he drove through the intersection, and she looked up, but by the time he had turned left into a market parking lot and driven back west on Santa Monica, she was nowhere to be seen.

He drove around several blocks, squinting as the winter sunlight shifted back and forth across the streaked windshield of his ten-year-old Honda, but none of the people on the sidewalks was her.

A couple of blocks south of Santa Monica he passed a fenced-off motel with plywood over its windows and several shopping carts in its otherwise empty parking lot. The 1960s space-age sign over the building read RO IC MOTEL, and he could see faint outlines where a long-gone T and P had once made "tropic" of the first word.

"Eroic," he said softly to himself.

To his own wry embarrassment he parked a block past it and fed his only quarter into the parking meter, but at the end of his twenty minutes she hadn't appeared.

Of course she hadn't. "You're acting like a high-school kid," he whispered impatiently to himself as he put the Honda in gear and pulled away from the curb.

●●

Six days later he was walking east toward Book City at Cherokee, and as was his habit lately he stepped into the Chinese Theater forecourt with three pennies in his hand, and he stood wearily beside the souvenir shop and scanned the crowd, shaking the pennies in his fist. The late afternoon crowd consisted of brightly dressed tourists, and a portly, bearded man making hats out of balloons, and several young men dressed as Batman and Spider-Man and Captain Jack Sparrow from the *Pirates of the Caribbean* movies.

Then he gripped the pennies tight. He saw her.

She was at the other end of the crowded square, on the far side of the theater entrance, and he noticed her red hair in the moment before she crouched out of sight.

He hurried through the crowd to where she was kneeling – the rains had passed and the pavement was dry – and he saw that she had laid three pennies into little round indentations in the Gregory Peck square.

She grinned up at him, squinting in the sunlight. "I love the idea," she said in the remembered husky voice, "but I didn't want to come between you and Jean Harlow." She reached up one narrow hand, and he took it gladly and pulled her to her feet. She could hardly weigh more than a hundred pounds. He realized that her hand was hot as he let go of it.

"And hello," she said.

She was wearing jeans and a gray sweatshirt again, or still. At least they were dry. Sydney caught again the scent of pears and cumin.

He was grinning too. Most of the books he sold he got from thrift stores and online used-book sellers, and these recent trips to Book City had been a self-respect excuse to keep looking for her here.

He groped for something to say. "I thought I found your 'Heroic' the other day," he told her.

She cocked her head, still smiling. The sweatshirt was baggy, but somehow she seemed to be flat-chested today. "You were looking for me?" she asked.

"I – guess I was. This was a closed-down motel, though, south of Santa Monica." He laughed self-consciously. "The sign says blank-R-O-blank-I-C. Eroic, see? It was originally Tropic, I gather."

Her green eyes had narrowed as he spoke, and it occurred to him that the condemned motel might actually be the place she'd referred to a couple of weeks earlier, and that she had not expected him to find it. "Probably it originally said 'erotic,'" she said lightly, taking his hand and stepping away from the Gregory Peck square. "Have you got a cigarette?"

"Yes." He pulled a pack of Camels and a lighter from his shirt pocket, and when she had tucked a cigarette between her lips – he noticed that she was not wearing lipstick today – he cupped his hand around the lighter and held the flame toward her. She held his hand to steady it as she puffed the cigarette alight.

"There couldn't be a motel called Erotic," he said.

"Sure there could, lover. To avoid complications."

"I'm George," he said. "What's your name?"

She shook her head, grinning up at him.

The bearded balloon man had shuffled across the pavement to them, deftly weaving a sort of bowler hat shape out of several long green balloons, and now he reached out and set it on her head.

"No, thank you," she said, taking it off and holding it toward the man, but he backed away, smiling through his beard and nodding. She stuck it onto the head of a little boy who was scampering past.

The balloon man stepped forward again and this time he snatched the cigarette from her mouth. "This is California, sister," he said, dropping it and stepping on it. "We don't smoke here."

"You should," she said, "it'd help you lose weight." She took Sydney's arm and started toward the sidewalk.

The balloon man called after them, "It's customary to give a gratuity for the balloons!"

"Get it from that kid," said Sydney over his shoulder.

The bearded man was pointing after them and saying loudly, "Tacky people, tacky people!"

"Could I have another cigarette?" she said as they stepped around the forecourt wall out of the shadows and started down the sunlit sidewalk toward the soft-drink and jewelry stands on the wider pavement in front of the Kodak Theater.

"Sure," said Sydney, pulling the pack and lighter out again. "Would you like a Coke or something?" he added, waving toward the nearest vendor. Their shadows stretched for yards ahead of them, but the day was still hot.

"I'd like a drink drink." She paused to take a cigarette, and again she put her hand over his as he lit it for her. "Drink, that knits up the raveled sleave of care," she said through smoke as they started forward again. "I bet you know where we could find a bar."

"I bet I do," he agreed. "Why don't you want to tell me your name?"

"I'm shy," she said. "What did the Michelin Man say, when we were leaving?"

"He said, 'tacky people.'"

She stopped and turned to look back, and for a moment Sydney was afraid she intended to march back and cause a scene; but a moment later she had grabbed his arm and resumed their eastward course.

He could feel that she was shaking, and he peered back over his shoulder.

Everyone on the pavement behind them seemed to be couples moving away or across his view, except for one silhouetted figure standing a hundred feet back – it was an elderly white-haired woman in a shapeless dress, and he couldn't see if she was looking after them or not.

The girl had released his arm and taken two steps ahead, and he started toward her –

– and she disappeared.

Sydney rocked to a halt.

He had been looking directly at her in the bright afternoon sunlight. She had not stepped into a store doorway or run on ahead or ducked behind him. She had been occupying volume four feet ahead of him, casting a shadow, and suddenly she was not.

A bus that had been grinding past on the far side of the parking meters to his left was still grinding past.

Her cigarette was rolling on the sidewalk, still lit.

She had not been a hallucination, and he had not experienced some kind of blackout.

Are you always so nice to dead people?

He was shivering in the sunlight, and he stepped back to half-sit against the rim of a black iron trash can by the curb. No sudden moves, he thought.

Was she a ghost? Probably, probably! What else?

Well then, you've seen a ghost, he told himself, that's all. People see ghosts. The balloon man saw her too – he told her not to smoke.

You fell in love with a ghost, that's all. People have probably done that.

He waited several minutes, gripping the iron rim of the trash can and glancing in all directions, but she didn't reappear.

At last he was able to push away from the trash can and walk on, unsteadily, toward Book City; that had been his plan before he had met her again today, and nothing else seemed appropriate. Breathing wasn't difficult, but for at least a little while it would be a conscious action, like putting one foot in front of the other.

He wondered if he would meet her again, knowing that she was a ghost. He wondered if he would be afraid of her now. He thought he probably would be, but he hoped he would see her again anyway.

●●

The quiet aisles of the book store, with the almost-vanilla scent of old paper, distanced him from the event on the sidewalk. This was his familiar world, as if all used book stores were actually one enormous magical building that you could enter through different doorways in Long Beach or Portland or Albuquerque. Always, reliably, there were the books with no spines that you had to pull out and identify, and the dust jackets that had to be checked for the dismissive words *Book Club Edition,* and the poetry section to be scanned for possibly underpriced Nora May French or George Sterling.

The shaking of his hands, and the disorientation that was like a half-second delay in his comprehension, were no worse than a hangover, and he was familiar with hangovers – the cure was a couple of drinks, and he would take the cure as soon as he got back to his apartment. In the meantime he was gratefully able to concentrate on the books, and within half an hour he had found several P. G. Wodehouse novels that he'd be able to sell for more than the prices they were marked at, and a clean five-dollar hardcover copy of Sabatini's *Bellarion.*

My books, he thought, and my poetry.

In the poetry section he found several signed Don Blanding books, but in his experience *every* Don Blanding book was signed. Then he found a first edition copy of Cheyenne Fleming's 1968 *More Poems,* but it was priced at twenty dollars, which was about the most it would ever go for. He looked on the title page for an inscription, but there wasn't one, and then flipped through the pages – and glimpsed handwriting.

He found the page again, and saw the name *Cheyenne Fleming* scrawled below one of the sonnets; and beside it was a thumbprint in the same fountain-pen ink.

He paused.

If this was a genuine Fleming signature, the book was worth about two hundred dollars. He was familiar with her poetry, but he didn't think he'd ever seen her signature; certainly he didn't have any signed Flemings at home to compare this against. But Christine would probably be able to say whether it was real or not – Christine Dunn was a book dealer he'd sometimes gone in with on substantial buys.

He'd risk the twenty dollars and call her when he got back to his apartment. And just for today he would walk straight north to Franklin, not west on Hollywood Boulevard. Not quite yet, not this evening.

••

His apartment building was on Franklin just west of Highland, a jacaranda-shaded old two-story horseshoe around an overgrown central courtyard, and supposedly Marlon Brando had stayed there before he'd become successful. Sydney's apartment was upstairs, and he locked the door after he had let himself into the curtained, tobacco-scented living room.

He poured himself a glass of bourbon from the bottle on the top kitchen shelf, and pulled a Coors from the refrigerator to chase the warm liquor with, and then he took his shopping bag to the shabby brown-leather chair in the corner and switched on the lamp.

It was of course the Fleming that interested him. He flipped open the book to the page with Fleming's name inked on it.

He recognized the sonnet from the first line – it was the rude sonnet to her sister...the sister who, he recalled, had become Fleming's literary executor after Fleming's suicide. Ironic.

He read the first eight lines of the sonnet, his gaze only bouncing over the lines since he had read it many times before:

> **To My Sister**
> *Rebecca, if your mirror were to show*
> *My face to you instead of yours, I wonder*

If you would notice right away, or know
The vain pretense you've chosen to live under.
If ever phone or doorbell rang, and then
I heard your voice conversing, what you'd say
Would be what I have said, recalled again,
And I might sit in silence through the day.

Then he frowned and took a careful sip of the bourbon. The last six lines weren't quite as he remembered them:

But when the Resurrection Man shall bring
The moon to free me from these yellowed pages,
The gift is mine, there won't be anything
For you — and you can rest through all the ages
Under a stone that bears the cherished name
You thought should make the two of us the same.

He picked up the telephone and punched in Christine's number.

After three rings he heard her say, briskly, "Dunn Books."

"Christine," he said, "George – uh – here." It was the first time he had spoken since seeing the girl disappear, and his voice had cracked. He cleared his throat and took a deep breath and let it out.

"Drunk again," said Christine.

"Again?" he said. "Still. Listen, I've got a first here of Fleming's *More Poems,* no dust jacket but it's got her name written below one of the poems. Do you have a signed Fleming I could compare it with?"

"You're in luck, an eBay customer backed out of a deal. It's a *More Poems,* too."

"Have you got it right there?"

"Yeah, but what, you want me to describe her signature over the phone? We should meet at the Biltmore tomorrow, bring our copies."

"Good idea, and if this is real I'll buy lunch. But could you flip to the sonnet 'To My Sister'?"

"One second." A few moments later she was back on the phone. "Okay, what about it?"

"How does the sestet go?"

"It says, *'But when the daylight of the future shows / The forms freed by erosion from their cages, / It will be mine that quickens, gladly grows, / And lives; and you can rest through all the ages / Under a stone that bears the cherished name / You thought should make the two of us the same.'* Bitter poem!"

Those were the familiar lines – the way the poem was supposed to go.

"Why," asked Christine, "is yours missing the bottom of the page?"

"No – I've – my copy has a partly different sestet." He read to her the last six lines on the page of the book he held. "Printed just like every other poem in the book, same typeface and all."

"Wow. Otherwise a standard copy of the first edition?"

"To the best of my knowledge, I don't know," he said, quoting a treasured remark from a bookseller they both knew. He added, "We'll know tomorrow."

"Eleven, okay? And take care of it – it might be worth wholesaling to one of the big-ticket dealers."

"I wasn't going to use it for a coaster. See you at eleven."

He hung up the phone, and before putting the book aside he touched the ink thumbprint beside the signature on the page. The paper wasn't warm or cold, but he shivered – this was a touch across decades. When had Fleming killed herself?

He got up and crossed the old carpets to the computer and turned it on, and as the monitor screen showed the Hewlett Packard logo and then the Windows background, he couldn't shake the mental image of trying to grab a woman to keep her from falling into some abyss and only managing to brush her outstretched hand with one finger.

He typed in the address for Google – *sounds like a Chinaman trying to say something* – and then typed "cheyenne fleming," and when a list of sites appeared he clicked on the top one. He had a dial-up AOL connection, so the text appeared first, flanking a square where a picture would soon appear.

Cheyenne Fleming, he read, had been born in Hollywood in 1934, and had lived there all her life with her younger sister Rebecca. Both had gone to UCLA, Cheyenne with more distinction than Rebecca, and both had published books of poetry, though Rebecca's had always been compared unfavorably with Cheyenne's. The sisters apparently both loved and resented each other, and the article quoted several lines from the "To My Sister" sonnet – the version Christine had read to him over the phone, not the version in his copy of *More Poems*. Cheyenne Fleming had shot herself in 1969, reportedly because Rebecca had stolen away her fiancée. Rebecca became her literary executor.

At last the picture appeared on the screen – it was black and white, but Sydney recognized the thin face with its narrow eyes and wide humorous mouth, and he knew that the disordered hair would be red in a color photograph.

The tip of his finger was numb where he had touched her thumbprint. *I'm Shy,* she had said. He had thought she was evading giving him her name. Shy for Cheyenne, of course. Pronounced Shy-*Ann*.

He glanced fearfully at his front door – what if she was standing on the landing out there right now, in the dusk shadows? He realized, with a shudder that made him carry his glass back to the kitchen for a refill, that he would open the door if she was – yes, and invite her in, invite her across his threshold. I finally fall in love, he thought, and it's with a dead woman. A suicide.

A line of black ants had found the coffee cup he'd left unwashed this morning, but he couldn't kill them right now.

Once his glass was filled again, he went to the living room window instead of the door, and he pulled the curtains aside. A huge orange full moon hung in the darkening sky behind the old TV antennas on the opposite roof. He looked down, but didn't see her among the shadowed trees and vines.

And in a Windingsheet of Vineleaf wrapped,
So bury me by some sweet Gardenside.

He closed the curtain and fetched the bottle and the twelve-pack of Coors to set beside his chair, then settled down to lose himself in one of the P. G. Wodehouse novels until he should be drunk enough to stumble to bed and fall instantly asleep.

••

As he trudged across Pershing Square from the parking structure on Hill Street toward the three imposing brown brick towers of the Biltmore Hotel, Sydney's squinting gaze kept being drawn in the direction of the new bright-yellow building on the south side of the square. His eyes were watering in the morning sun-glare anyway, and he wondered irritably why somebody would paint a new building in that idiotic kindergarten color.

He had awakened early, and his hangover seemed to be just a continuation of his disorientation from the day before. He had decided that he couldn't sell the Fleming book. Even though he had met her two weeks before finding the book, he was certain that the book was somehow his link to her.

Christine would be disappointed – part of the fun of bookselling was writing catalogue copy for extraordinary items, and she would have wanted to collaborate in the description of this item – but he couldn't help that.

His gaze was drawn again toward the yellow building, but now that he was closer to it he could see that it wasn't the building that his eyes had been drawn toward, but a stairway and pool just this side of it. Two six-foot brown stone spheres were mounted on the pool coping.

And he saw her sitting down there, on the shady side of one of the giant stone balls.

He was smiling and stepping across the pavement in that direction even before he was sure it was her, and the memory, only momentarily delayed, of who she must be didn't slow his pace.

She was wearing the jeans and sweatshirt again, and she stood up and waved at him when he was still a hundred feet away, and even at this distance he was sure he caught her pears-and-cumin scent.

He sprinted the last few yards, and her arms were wide so he hugged her when they met.

"George," she said breathily in his ear. The fruit-and-spice smell was strong.

"Shy," he said, and hugged her more tightly. He could feel her breastbone against his, and he wondered if she had been wearing a padded bra when he had first seen her. Then he held her by her shoulders at arm's length and smiled into her squinting, elfin eyes. "I've got to make a call," he said.

He pulled his cell phone out of his jacket pocket, flipped it open and tapped in Christine's well-remembered number. He was already ten minutes late for their meeting.

"Christine," he said, "I've got to beg off…no, I'm not going to be home. I'm going to be in Orange County –"

Cheyenne mouthed *Overnight*.

"– overnight," Sydney went on, "till tomorrow. No, I…I'll explain it later, and I owe you a lunch. No, I haven't sold it yet! I gotta run, I'm in traffic and I can't drive and talk at the same time. Right, right – 'bye!"

He folded it and tucked it back into his pocket.

Cheyenne nodded. "To avoid complications," she said.

Sydney had stepped back from her, but he was holding her hand – possibly to keep her from disappearing again. "My New Year's resolution," he said with a rueful smile, "was not to tell any lies."

"My attitude toward New Year's resolutions is the same as Oscar Wilde's," she said, stepping around the pool coping and swinging his hand.

"What did he say about them?" asked Sydney, falling into step beside her.

"I don't know if he ever said anything about them," she said, "but if he did, I'm sure I agree with it."

She looked back at him, then glanced past him and lost her smile.

"Don't turn around," she said quickly, so he just stared at her face, which seemed bony and starved between the wings of tangled red hair. "Now look around, but scan the whole square, like you're calculating if they could land the Goodyear blimp here."

Sydney let his gaze swivel from Hill Street, across the trees and broad pavement of the square, to the pillared arch of the Biltmore entrance. Up there toward the east end of the square he had seen a gray-haired woman in a loose blue dress; she seemed to be the same woman he had seen behind them on Hollywood Boulevard yesterday.

He let his eyes come back around to focus on Cheyenne's face.

"You saw that woman?" she said to him. "The one that looks like…

some kind of featherless monkey? Stay away from her, she'll tell you lies about me."

Looking at the Biltmore entrance had reminded him that Christine might have parked in the Hill Street lot too. "Let's sit behind one of these balls," he said. And when they had walked down the steps and sat on the cement coping, leaning back against the receding under-curve of the nearest stone sphere, he said, "I found your book. I hope you don't mind that I know who you are."

She was still holding his hand, and now she squeezed it. "Who am I, lover?"

"You're Cheyenne Fleming. You – you're –"

"Yes. How did I die?"

He took a deep breath. "You killed yourself."

"I did? Why?"

"Because your sister – I read – ran off with your fiancée."

She closed her eyes and twined her fingers through his. "Urbane legends. Can I come over to your place tonight? I want to copy one of my poems in the book, write it out again in the blank space around the printed version, and I need you to hold my hand, guide my hand while I write it."

"Okay," he said. His heart was thudding in his chest. Inviting her over my threshold, he thought. "I'd like that," he added with dizzy bravado.

"I've got the pen to use," she went on. "It's my special pen, they buried me with it."

"Okay." Buried her with it, he thought. Buried her with it.

"I love you," she said, her eyes still closed. "Do you love me? Tell me you love me."

He was sitting down, but his head was spinning with vertigo as if an infinite black gulf yawned at his feet. This was her inviting *him* over *her* threshold.

"Under," he said in a shaky voice, "normal circumstances, I'd certainly be in love with you."

"Nobody falls in love under *normal* circumstances," she said softly, rubbing his finger with her warm thumb. He restrained an impulse to look to see if there was still ink on it. "Love isn't in the category of normal things. Not any worthwhile kind of love, anyway." She opened her eyes and waved her free hand behind them toward the square. "Normal people. I hate them."

"Me too," said Sydney.

"Actually," she said, looking down at their linked hands, "I didn't kill myself." She paused for so long that he was about to ask her what had happened, when she went on quietly, "My sister Rebecca shot me, and made it look like a suicide. After that she apparently *did* go away with my fiancée. But she killed me because she had made herself into an imitation of me, and without me in the picture, *she'd* be the original." Through her hand he felt her shiver. "I've been alone in the dark for a long time," she said in a small voice.

Sydney freed his hand so that he could put his arm around her narrow shoulders, and he kissed her hair.

Cheyenne looked up with a grin that made slits of her eyes. "But I don't think she's prospered! Doesn't she look *terrible?*"

Sydney resisted the impulse to look around again. "Was that –"

Cheyenne frowned. "I've got to go – I can't stay here for very long at a time, not until we copy that poem."

She kissed him, and their mouths opened, and for a moment his tongue touched hers. When their lips parted their foreheads were pressed together, and he whispered, "Let's get that poem copied, then."

She smiled, deepening the lines in her cheeks, and looked down. "Sit back now and look away from me," she said. "And I'll come to your place tonight."

He pressed his palms against the surface of the cement coping and pushed himself away from her, and looked toward Hill Street.

After a moment, "Shy?" he said; and when he looked around she was gone. "I love you," he said to the empty air.

"Everybody did," came a raspy voice from behind and above him.

For a moment he went on staring at the place where Cheyenne had sat; then he sighed deeply and looked around.

The old woman in the blue dress was standing at the top of the stairs, and now began stepping carefully down them in boxy old-lady shoes.

Her eyes were pouchy above round cheeks and not much of a chin, and Sydney imagined she'd been cute decades ago.

"Are," he said in a voice he made himself keep level, "you Rebecca?"

She stopped in front of him and nodded, frowning in the sun-glare. "Rebecca Fleming," she said. "The cherished name." The diesel-scented breeze was blowing her white hair around her face, and she pushed it back with one frail, spotted hand. "Did she say I killed her?"

After a moment's hesitation, "Yes," Sydney said.

She sat down, far enough away from him that he didn't feel called on to move further away. Why hadn't he brought a flask?

"True," she said, exhaling as if she'd been holding her breath. "True, I did." She looked across at him, and he reluctantly met her eyes. They were green, just like Cheyenne's.

"I bet," she said, "you bought a book of hers, signed." She barked two syllables of a laugh. "And I bet she's still got her fountain pen. We buried it with her."

"I don't think you and I have much to say to each other," said Sydney stiffly. He started to get to his feet.

"It was self-defense, if you're curious," she said, not stirring.

He paused, bracing himself on his hands.

"She came into my room," said Rebecca, "with a revolver. I woke up when she touched the cold muzzle to my forehead. This is thirty-seven years ago, but I remember it as if it were last night – we were in a crummy motel south of Santa Monica Boulevard, on one of her low-life tours. I sat up and pushed the gun away, but she kept trying to get it aimed at me – she was laughing, irritated, cajoling, I wasn't playing along properly – and when I pushed it back toward her it went off. Under her chin. I wrote a suicide note for her."

The old woman's face was stony. Sydney sat back down.

"I loved her," she said. "If I'd known that resisting her would end up killing her, I swear, I wouldn't have resisted." She smiled at him belligerently. "Crush an ant sometime, and then smell your fingers. I wonder what became of the clothes we buried her in. Not a sweatshirt and jeans."

"A black linen suit," said Sydney, "with a white blouse. They were damp."

"Well, groundwater, you know, even with a cement grave-liner. And a padded bra, for the photographs. I fixed it up myself, crying so hard I could barely see the stitches – I filled the lining with bird-seed to flesh her out."

Sydney recalled the vines that had seemed to be embroidered on Cheyenne's bra, that first day. "It sprouted."

Rebecca laughed softly. "'Quickens, gladly grows.' She wants something from you." Rebecca fumbled in a pocket of her skirt. "Bring the moon to free her from these yellowed pages."

Sydney squinted at her. "You've read that version of the sonnet?"

Rebecca was now holding out a two-inch clear plastic cylinder with metal bands on it. "I was there when she wrote it. She read it to me when the ink was still wet. It was printed that way in only one copy of the book, the copy you obviously found, God help us all. This is one of her ink cartridges. You stick this end in the ink bottle and twist the other end – that retracts the plunger. When she was writing poetry she used to use about nine parts Scheaffer's black ink and one part her own blood."

She was still holding it toward him, so he took it from her.

"The signature in your book certainly contains some of her blood," Rebecca said.

"A signature and a thumbprint," said Sydney absently, rolling the narrow cylinder in his palm. He twisted the back end, and saw the tiny red ring of the plunger move smoothly up the inside of the clear barrel.

"And you touched the thumbprint."

"Yes. I'm glad I did."

"You brought her to this cycle of the moon. She arrived on the new moon, though you probably didn't find the book and touch her thumb till further on in the cycle; she'd instantly stain the whole twenty-eight days, I'm sure, backward and forward. Do you know yet what she wants you to do?"

If I'd known, Rebecca had said, *that resisting her would end up killing her, I swear, I wouldn't have resisted.* Sydney realized, to his dismay, that he believed her.

"Hold her hand, guide it, I guess, while she copies a poem," he said.

"*That* poem, I have no doubt. She's a ghost – I suppose she imagines that writing it again will project her spirit back to the night when she originally wrote it – so she can make a better attempt at killing me three years later, in 1969. She was thirty-five, in '69. I was thirty-three."

"She looks younger."

"She always did. See little Shy riding horseback, you'd think she was twelve years old." Rebecca sat back. "She's pretty physical, right? I mean, she can hold things, touch things?"

Sydney remembered Cheyenne's fingers intertwined with his.

"Yes."

"I'd think she could hold a pen. I wonder why she needs help copying the poem."

"I –" Sydney began.

But Rebecca interrupted him. "If you do it for her," she said, "and it works, she won't have died. I'll be the one that died in '69. She'll be seventy-two now, and you won't have met her. Well, she'll probably look you up, if she remembers to be grateful, but you won't remember any of…this interlude with her." She smiled wryly. "And you certainly won't meet me. That's a plus, I imagine. Do you have any high-proof liquor, at your house?"

"You can't come over!" said Sydney, appalled.

"No, I wasn't thinking of that. Never mind. But you might ask her –"

She had paused, and Sydney raised his eyebrows.

"You might ask her not to kill me, when she gets back there. I know I'd have left, moved out, if she had told me she really needed that. I'd have stopped…trying to *be* her. I only did it because I loved her." She smiled, and for a moment as she stood up Sydney could see that she must once have been very pretty.

"Goodbye, Resurrection Man," she said, and turned and shuffled away up the cement steps.

Sydney didn't call after her. After a moment he realized that he was still holding the plastic ink-cartridge, and he put it in his pocket.

High-proof liquor, he thought unhappily.

●●

Back in his apartment after making a couple of purchases, he poured himself a shot of bourbon from the kitchen bottle and sat down by the window with the Fleming book.

> *But when the Resurrection Man shall bring*
> *The moon to free me from these yellowed pages,*
> *The gift is mine, there won't be anything*
> *For you.*

The moon had been full last night. Or maybe just a hair short of full, and it would be full tonight.

You might ask her not to kill me, when she gets back there.

He opened the bags he had carried home from a liquor store and a stationer's, and he pulled the ink cartridge out of his pocket.

One bag contained a squat glass bottle of Scheaffer's black ink, and he unscrewed the lid; there was a little pool of ink in the well on the inside of the open bottle's rim, and he stuck the end of the cartridge into the ink and twisted the back. The plunger retracted, and the barrel ahead of it was black.

When it was a third filled, he stopped, and he opened the other bag. It contained a tiny plastic 50-milliliter bottle – what he thought of as breakfast-sized – of Bacardi 151-proof rum. He twisted off the cap and stuck the cartridge into the vapory liquor. He twisted the end of the cartridge until it stopped, filled, and even though the cylinder now contained two-thirds rum, it was still jet-black.

He had considered buying lighter-fluid, but decided that the 151-proof rum – seventy-five percent alcohol – would probably be more flammable. And he could drink what he didn't use.

●●

He was dozing in the chair when he heard someone moving in the kitchen. He sat up, disoriented, and hoarsely called, "Who's there?"

He lurched to his feet, catching the book but missing the tiny empty rum bottle.

"Who were you expecting, lover?" came Cheyenne's husky voice. "Should I have knocked? You already invited me."

He stumbled across the dim living room into the kitchen. The overhead light was on in there, and through the little kitchen window he saw that it was dark outside.

Cheyenne was sweeping the last of the ants off the counter with her hand, and as he watched she rubbed them vigorously between her palms and wiped her open hands along her jaw and neck, then picked up the half-full bourbon bottle.

She was wearing the black linen skirt and jacket again – and, he could see, the birdseed-sprouting bra under the white blouse. The clothes were somehow still damp.

"I talked to Rebecca," he blurted, thinking about the ink cartridge in his pocket.

"I told you not to," she said absently. "Where do you keep glasses? Or do you expect me to drink right out of the bottle? Did she say she killed me in self-defense?"

"Yes."

"Glasses?"

He stepped past her and opened a cupboard and handed her an Old Fashioned glass. "Yes," he said again.

She smiled up at him from beneath her dark eyelashes as she poured a couple of ounces of amber liquor into the glass, then put down the bottle and caressed his cheek. The fruit-and-spice smell of crushed ants was strong.

"It was my fault!" she said, laughing as she spoke. "I shouldn't have touched her with the barrel! And so it was little Shy that wound up getting killed, miserabile dictu! I was...*nonplussed* in eternity." She took a deep sip of the bourbon and then sang, "'Take my hand, I'm nonplussed in eternity...'"

He wasn't smiling, so she pushed out her thin red lips. "Oh, lover, don't pout. Am I my sister's keeper? Did you know she claimed I got my best poems by stealing her ideas? As if anybody couldn't tell from reading *her* poetry which of us was the original! At least I had already got that copy of my book out there, out in the world, like a message in a bottle, a soul in a bottle, for you to eventually –"

Sydney had held up his hand, and she stopped. "She said to tell you... not to kill her. She said she'd just move out if you asked her to. If she knew it was important to you."

She shrugged. "Maybe."

He frowned and took a breath, but she spoke again before he could.

"Are you still going to help me copy out my poem? I can't write it by myself, because the first word of it is the name of the person who killed me."

Her eyes were wide and her eyebrows were raised as she looked down at the book in his hand and then back up at him.

"I'd do it for you," she added softly, "because I love you. Do you love me?"

She couldn't be taller than five-foot one-inch, and with her long neck and thin arms, and her big eyes under the disordered hair, she looked young and frail.

"Yes," he said. I do, he thought. And I'm going to exorcise you. I'm going to spread that flammable ink-and-rum mix over the page and then touch it with a cigarette.

It was printed that way in only one copy of the book, Rebecca had said, *the copy you obviously found, God help us all.* A soul in a bottle.

There won't be another Resurrection Man.

He made himself smile. "You've got a pen, you said."

She reached thin fingers into the neck of her blouse and pulled out a long, tapering black pen. She shook it to dislodge a thin white tendril with a tiny green leaf on it.

"May I?" he asked, holding out his hand.

She hesitated, then laid the pen in his palm.

He handed her the book, then pulled off the pen's cap, exposing the gleaming, wedge-shaped nib. "Do you need to dip it in an ink bottle?" he asked.

"No, it's got a cartridge in it. Unscrew the end."

He twisted the barrel and the nib-end rotated away from the pen, and after a few more turns it came loose in his hand, exposing a duplicate of the ink-cartridge he had in his pocket.

"Pull the cartridge off," she said suddenly, "and lick the end of it. Didn't she tell you about my ink?"

"No," he said, his voice unsteady. "Tell me about your ink."

"Well, it's got a little bit of my blood in it, though it's mostly ink." She was flipping through the pages of the book. "But some blood. Lick it, the punctured end of the cartridge." She looked up at him and grinned. "As a chaser for the rum I smell on your breath."

For ten seconds he stared into her deep green eyes, then he raised the cartridge and ran his tongue across the end of it. He didn't taste anything.

"That's my dear man," she said, taking his hand and stepping onto the living room carpet. "Let's sit in that chair you were napping in."

As they crossed the living room, Sydney slid his free hand into his pocket and clasped the rum-and-ink cartridge next to the blood-and-ink one. The one he had prepared this afternoon was up by his knuckles, the other at the base of his palm.

She let go of his hand to reach out and switch on the lamp, and Sydney pulled a pack of Camels out of his shirt pocket and shook one free.

"Sit down," she said, "I'll sit in your lap. I hardly weigh anything. Are there limits to what you'd do for someone you love?"

Sydney hooked a cigarette onto his lip and tossed the pack aside. "Limits?" he said as he sat down and clicked a lighter at the end of the cigarette. "I don't know," he said around a puff of smoke.

"I think you're not one of those normal people," she said.

"I hate 'em." He laid his cigarette in the smoking stand beside the chair.

"Me too," she said, and she slid onto his lap and curled her left arm around his shoulders. Her skirt and sleeve were damp, but not cold.

With her right hand she opened the book to the sonnet "To My Sister."

"Lots of margin space for us to write in," she said.

Her hot cheek was touching his, and when he turned to look at her he found that he was kissing her, gently at first and then passionately, for this moment not caring that her scent was the smell of crushed ants.

"Put the cartridge," she whispered into his mouth, "back into the pen and screw it closed."

He carefully fitted one of the cartridges into the pen and whirled the base until it was tight.

••

George Sydney stood up from crouching beside the shelf of cookbooks, holding a copy of James Beard's *On Food*. It was his favorite of Beard's books, and if he couldn't sell it at a profit he'd happily keep it.

He hadn't found any other likely books here today, and now it was nearly noon and time to walk across the boulevard to Boardner's for a couple of quick drinks.

"There he is," said the man behind the counter and the cash register. "George, this lady has been coming in every day for the last week, looking for you."

Sydney blinked toward the brightly sunlit store windows, and in front of the counter he saw the silhouette of a short elderly woman with a halo of back-lit white hair.

He smiled and shuffled forward. "Well, hi," he said.

"Hello, George," she said in a husky voice, holding out her hand.

He stepped across the remaining distance and shook her hand. "What —" he began.

"I was just on my way to the Chinese Theater," she said. She was smiling up at him almost sadly, and though her face was deeply etched with wrinkles, her green eyes were lively and young. "I'm going to lay three pennies in the indentations in Gregory Peck's square."

He laughed in surprise. "I do that with Jean Harlow!"

"That's where I got the idea." She leaned forward and tipped her face up and kissed him briefly on the lips, and he dropped the James Beard book.

He crouched to retrieve the book, and when he straightened up she had already stepped out the door. He saw her walking away west down Hollywood Boulevard, her white hair fluttering around her head in the wind.

The man behind the counter was middle-aged, with a graying moustache. "Do you know who your admirer is, George?" he asked with a kinked smile.

Sydney had taken a step toward the door, but some misgiving made him stop. He exhaled to clear his head of a sharp sweet, musty scent.

"Uh," he said distractedly, "no. Who is she?"

"That was Cheyenne Fleming. I got her to sign some copies of her books the other day, so I can double the prices."

"I thought she was dead by now." Sydney tried to remember what he'd read about Fleming. "When was it she got paroled?"

"I don't know. In the '80s? Some time after the death penalty was repealed in the '70s, anyway." He waved at a stack of half a dozen slim dark books on the desk behind him. "You want one of the signed ones? I'll let you have it for the original price, since she only came in here looking for you."

Sydney looked at the stack.

"Nah," he said, pushing the James Beard across the counter. "Just this."

A few moments later he was outside on the brass-starred sidewalk, squinting after Cheyenne Fleming. He could see her, a hundred feet away to the west now, striding away.

He rubbed his face, trying to get rid of the odd scent. And as he walked away, east, he wondered why that kiss should have left him feeling dirty, as if it had been a mortal sin for which he couldn't now phrase the need for absolution.

●●●

This story originated in my frustration that the poet Edna St. Vincent Millay died two years before I was born. The character Cheyenne Fleming deviated from Millay by becoming, I'm afraid, a much less interesting person than her original model – certainly poor Fleming's sonnets can't hold a candle (lit at both ends or not) to Millay's! But then I think Millay was the best sonnetist since Shakespeare, so I guess Fleming shouldn't feel too bad.

It was an entertaining chore for me to write sonnets — one in the story, and three for inclusion in the limited edition from Subterranean Press — from the point of view of a fictional character, and so later I did it again with the protagonist of the novel Three Days to Never.

The incident with the balloon man in the forecourt of the Chinese Theater really happened, and it was my wife who had the cigarette snatched from her mouth; the man was wearing a top hat, and she knocked it off. The used-book store, Book City, isn't there anymore, unfortunately.

—T. P.

The Hour of Babel

•••

A gust of rainy wind wobbled the old 350 Honda as it made a right turn from Anaheim Boulevard into the empty parking lot, but the rider swerved a little wider to correct for it, and the green neutral-light shone under the water-beaded plastic window of the speedometer gauge as he coasted to a stop in one of the parking spaces in front of the anonymous office building.

He flipped down the kickstand and let the bike lean onto it without touching his shoe to the gleaming black pavement, and he unsnapped his helmet and pulled it off, shaking out his gray hair as he stared at the three-story building. In sunlight its white stucco walls were probably bright, but on this overcast noon it just looked ashen.

He shifted around on the plastic shopping bag he had draped over the section of black steel frame where the padded seat had once been, and squinted across the street. Past the wet cars hissing by in both directions he could see the bar, though it had a different name now. Probably the last person he knew from those days had quit going in there twenty years ago.

He looked back at the office building in front of him and tried to remember the Firehouse Pizza building that had stood there in 1975. It had sat further back, it seemed to him, with a wider parking lot in front.

The spot where he used to park his bike was somewhere inside this new building now.

He reached a gloved hand below the front of the gas tank and switched off the engine.

••

"Is he coming in?"

The bald man at the computer monitor stared at the red dot on the map-grid. "I don't –"

"Look out the window," said Hartford Evian with exaggerated clarity.

"Oh, right." Scarbee got up from the computer and crossed to the tinted window that overlooked Anaheim Boulevard, and peered down. "He's just sitting on his motorcycle, with his helmet off." He rubbed his nose. "It's raining."

"Was this visit on the schedule?"

"I suppose so. Why should they show *me* the schedule? It must have been."

Evian had flipped open a cell phone and begun awkwardly punching numbers into it, when Scarbee added, "Now Kokolo just drove in."

Evian swore and quickly finished pushing the tiny buttons.

"Perry," he said a moment later, "don't look at the guy on the motorcycle to your right, it's Hollis. *Hollis*. Yes, that one. It's not on any schedule *I* ever saw. Just walk in, ignore him." After listening for a moment, he went on, "Wait, wait! Felise is with you? Tell Felise not to get out of the car!"

Scarbee was still looking out the window. "Felise is already out of the car," he said.

"Get in here, both of you, quick, don't look around," said Evian, and then he snapped the phone closed. "Did Hollis look at her?"

"Well," said Scarbee, "he looked over at both of them."

Evian opened his mouth as if to speak, hesitated, then said, "Call Hoag Hospital. We've got to get Lyle back here right now, not later today."

Scarbee turned around to face the desk. "That's earlier than we said. His doctors won't –"

"Keep watching Hollis!" When Scarbee turned back to the window, Evian said, "They'll go along if Lyle insists. I'm sure that's what happens. Tell him we'll give his family more money. Double."

"I hope they've got an ambulance free, to drive all the way here from Newport. Now he's putting his helmet back on. Hollis, down there."

Evian hit a button on the intercom. "You guys see the biker out front?" he asked.

"We see him," came a woman's voice from the speaker.

Scarbee said, "I think he's trying to start his motorcycle. It looks like he's jumping on it."

"Get him inside," said Evian, "polite if possible." He released the button.

A moment later Scarbee said, "Couple of security guys, running out. And – huh! I think they just stun-gunned him. Now they're walking him back in, but I think he's unconscious. His motorcycle fell over."

"Not very polite." Evian stood up and ran his fingers through his graying hair. "Now I guess we all talk to Hollis. I swear this wasn't in the goddamn schedule! Get him into the conference room – and remind them to be sure the area of measurement is locked. And get somebody to prop his silly motorcycle up again."

••

Kurt Hollis was still shaky and nauseated, but he sat back and sighed when the bald man slid a bowl of M&Ms across the table toward him. Hollis looked past the four people on the other side of the table at the windows high in the white cinder-block wall, then glanced at the two men standing by the door behind him.

At last he focused on the four people sitting across from him. Two of them he had seen a few minutes ago in the parking lot – the dark-haired young woman in a lumberjack shirt with the sleeves rolled back, and the blond man in a silver-fabric windbreaker. All the other men were in jackets and ties.

The bald man waved at the M&Ms. "The electric shock made your muscles go into rapid spasms," he said. "All your blood sugar was converted to lactic acid."

Hollis stared at him, and the bald man looked at the ceiling, apparently reconsidering what he had said. "You should eat these...candies," he said finally.

"Cigarettes," said Hollis. It was the first time he had spoken in several days, and his voice was hoarse. He spread his hand, then slowly reached into his damp brown leather jacket and pulled out a crumpled pack of Camels and hooked a Bic lighter out of one side of it.

"Smoking!" said the bald man. "No, you can't use those in here."

Hollis let go of the cigarette pack and the lighter. "You've mistaken me for somebody," he said. "Check it out. Let me go and this whole thing is just my word against yours."

The blond man in the silver windbreaker leaned forward. "You are Kurt Hollis," he said, "fifty-one years old, apartment on 16th Street in Santa Ana."

The gray-haired man beside him shifted in his chair and said, "We think you recognized Felise here." He waved at the young lady.

Hollis stared at her. Fluorescent lights in the ceiling were bright

54

enough for him to see her clearly against the muted gray daylight from the windows.

"No," he said. "And I don't know anybody named Felise. I'm Kurt Hollis, but you've got crossed wires somewhere." He rubbed his eyes, then dropped his hands to the tabletop and tucked the lighter back into the cigarette pack. "I'm going to walk out of here," he said, shifting his chair back on the carpet. "Where'd you put my helmet?"

Felise reached out and took a handful of the M&Ms. "You can't possibly eat all of them," she said, and her voice was light and amused.

And Hollis recognized her.

"Liquor," he said, and reached into his jacket again, to pull out a flat half-pint bottle of Wild Turkey bourbon. His hand was shaking now as he unscrewed the cap and tilted the bottle up for a mouthful.

••

In 1975 he had been twenty years old, working at Firehouse Pizza until late June, and one weekday night in April he had been clearing away the litter a departed family had left on one of the picnic tables out in the dining area, when a dark-haired young woman sitting by herself at a nearby table had said, "Hey."

Hollis had turned to look at her. "Hey." She had seemed to be about his age, possibly a year or two younger.

He could remember the smells of the place, even now – the sharp reek of tomato sauce and garlic, the stale smell of the beer-soaked wood-slat floor behind the bar, the harsh odor of the ashtrays on all the tables.

She had nodded toward the aluminum pizza pans he had picked up. "What happens to the pizzas people don't finish?"

Hollis looked down at the pans. Several triangular slices of pizza had been left uneaten, pepperoni in one pan and sausage and bell pepper in the other.

"We just throw 'em out," he said. "Hard luck on the starving children in China, but…that's what we do."

"Oh," she said. "I wondered."

Hollis hesitated, then glanced to the bar and back to her. "Sometimes I leave them at the end of the bar," he said. "Till I have time to take them to the back room, where the sinks are."

After another pause, he nodded and carried the pans to the bar, and set them in front of one of the empty stools on the side of the cash register away from the kitchen. There were no customers at the bar, so he walked on into the kitchen, where two other young men in aprons and red-and-white-striped shirts were listlessly painting tomato sauce onto disks of dough. Hollis took the long-handled spatula from the top of the oven and pulled open the narrow top door – probably he had burned his forearm on the door-edge, as he often did – and turned the pizzas that sat on the flour-dusted iron floor inside.

When he looked through the doorway to the bar a few minutes later, he saw the girl sitting at the end of the bar, chewing. When he looked again, she was gone, and later when he went to pick up the pans he saw that they were empty.

Hollis and the girl never spoke again, though she had come in about once a week, always on a slow weekday night, and sat at the stool beyond the cash register, and Hollis had every time found an opportunity to leave a half-finished pizza or two near her.

And she had been there, he recalled now, on that last night, June 21, 1975; the night Firehouse Pizza closed down, and he had thus lost the last real job he'd ever had; the night that had been intruding so stressfully into his dreams lately that he had actually ridden his bike over here today. The night of which he had no recollection past about 8 PM, though he had awakened the next day at noon in his apartment, his face stiff with dried tears and stinging with impossible sunburn.

••

You can't possibly eat all of them.

He stared at her now as she sat chewing M&Ms across the table from him, stared at the corners of her eyes, the skin on her throat and the backs of her hands. It was all still smooth – she still looked to be about twenty years old.

"That," he said carefully, "was thirty-one years ago. A bit more."

"That's recommended retail time," she said. "We get it wholesale."

"You do recognize her," said the blond man.

"Who are these guys?" Hollis asked Felise. "Why is he wearing that Buck Rogers jacket?"

"It's a uniform," said Felise, "or will be. Could I – ?" she added, with a wave toward the bottle of Wild Turkey. When Hollis nodded she reached over and slid it to her side and took a sip from it. "But I've got to admit," she said, exhaling around the whiskey, "that it makes him look like a baked potato that was taken too young from its mother."

"My name is Perry Kokolo," the blond man said, apparently unruffled. "The citizens beside me are Hartford Evian and Zip Scarbee. We employ Felise as a consultant. Do you remember a man named Don Lyle?"

"Yes!" Don had been working that night too, Hollis recalled now. The boss had left for the night, and he and Don had been drinking beers as they worked, pausing occasionally to sing old Dean Martin songs over the loudspeaker that was meant for calling out pick-up numbers.

"He'll be joining us soon," Kokolo went on. "He's done some consulting for us too, on a more freelance basis. We'd like your help as well."

"They pay very nice," said Felise. "I can afford my own pizzas now."

"Did they recruit you with a stun-gun?"

Felise said, "Probably," as gray-haired Evian said, "Apologies, apologies! It was urgent, our people got carried away. And we do pay well."

"Help...with what?" asked Hollis.

"We simply want to find out what happened here on June 21, 1975."

"The night God vomited on Firehouse Pizza," said Felise, nodding solemnly.

Hollis took a deep breath and let it out. "I don't remember anything about that night after about eight." He looked at the four people across from him. "Why is it important? Now?"

"You're finally starting to remember, I think," said Evian. "You drove your motorcycle here today, and you recognized Felise, eventually. As to why it's important —"

"They can't," interrupted Felise, "we can't, that is, time-travel to that night. They can't get closer than a half hour on either side of it, and if they get there early and then try to walk in, they find they're walking out. Without changing direction. Even me, and I'm already *in* there."

The bald man, Scarbee, spoke up: "Cameras we leave in there disappear on that evening."

"It's like an island in the time stream," agreed Evian. "We're confined to the metaphorical water, and so we find we've gone by the incident, or we're short of it, but we can't get *to* it. And something important happened then. Then by there, I mean."

Felise said, "He means 'then and there.'"

"Time-travel," said Hollis flatly. He took the bourbon bottle and drank a mouthful, then glanced around at the featureless room.

"Congress approved a new super-collider in Dallas in 2012," said the bald-headed man, "and the National Security Agency got Fermilab in Chicago. Charged tachyons in a mile-wide magnetic ring. It can project power fifth-dimensionally for a range of about fifty years back and twenty forward – there's some kind of Lorentzian ether headwind. We get shut down in 2019."

Hollis frowned and opened his mouth, but before he could speak, Felise said, "It's true. Look at me."

For several seconds none of them spoke.

"So," said Hollis finally, with no expression, "you can change the past?"

"Apparently not," said Evian. "But we can usually find out what it is. What happened that night?"

"Ask Felise," said Hollis, "or Don. They were both there too, then. Thex."

"I hid behind the bar," said Felise, "after the devil's hula-hoops and basketballs started spinning."

Hollis's forehead was suddenly cold with sweat. *That's right*, he thought – *hoops and balls*.

The deteriorating scar wall he had built up around the memory had been severely shaken by seeing Felise again, still as young as she had been on that night, and now, with this prompt from her, it gave way at last.

He had been on the phone by the front cash register when his vision had begun to flicker – he had been looking out past the counter at the tables, but suddenly without shifting his head he had seen curled segments of the pinball machines at the back end of the dining room, and even of the dumpster out back.

And then the spheres and rings had appeared in the air, rapidly expanding and sending tables flying in a clatter, or shrinking down to nothing. They were zebra-patterned in black and silver, and the stripes shifted as rapidly as the size of the impossible things.

Probably the intrusion had lasted no more than ten seconds. Five.

There had never been any police investigation later, but people had died there. Hollis could remember seeing a man explosively crushed against one of the walls as an expanding ring punched most of his body right through into the alley.

••

How could I have forgotten this? he thought now; how could I *not* have forgotten it?

And then he seemed to recall that he had met it —

Only after he choked on warm bourbon did he realize that he had snatched up the bottle. He coughed, and then drank what remained in three heroic gulps.

"It was a hallucination," he said hoarsely, wondering if he was going to be sick. "There would have been cops, ambulances —"

"Yes," said Evian, "if we hadn't stepped in and asserted national security. Pre-emptive jurisdiction. Nerve gas, terrorists, plausible enough. We were in place around the building and had it cordoned off even before the first survivor came out."

"That was me, I think," said Felise with a visible shiver. "And I think you guys *did* stun-gun me, now that I think of it." She gave Hollis a haunted look. "It's only six months ago, for me."

"What," said Evian, leaning forward, "was it?"

"It was silver-and-black balls," snapped Hollis, "and donut-shaped things, that busted the place up and killed people."

"Silver and black," whispered Felise, nodding.

"What did it say?"

Hollis's chest was suddenly cold, and his hands were tingling, and he couldn't take a deep breath.

"Say? It didn't *say* anything! Good God!"

Had it *said* anything?

"It didn't say anything," said Felise, still whispering, "I swear."

"What do you think you...*learned* from it?"

"Nothing," said Hollis. "Stay out of pizza parlors."

Evian smiled. "When's the last time you've seen a doctor, got a, a check-up?"

"What, radiation? After thirty-one years?" When Evian just continued to smile at him, Hollis thought about it. "When I was in college, I guess."

"That's a long time."

Hollis shrugged. "All I want to hear from a doctor is, 'If you had come in six months ago we could have done something about this.'"

"You were going to college, but you never went again after that night."

"Sure. What's the use of knowing anything?"

"And you've never married."

"I don't know any women well enough to hate 'em that much."

Felise laughed with apparent delight. "Lyle says the same thing! It was redundant for that thing to crush people *physically.*"

Evian went on, "I gather you share Felise's opinion that it was one thing, that appeared as a lot of inconstant shapes?"

Hollis sighed deeply. "You guys actually know something about... all that?"

"We've been looking into it for thirty years," said Evian.

"Across thirty years, anyway," said Felise.

Hollis rubbed his face. "Yes," he said, then lowered his hands and looked down at them. "It was one thing. It...passed through our, our what, our space, like somebody diving into a pond through a carpet of water lilies. If the diver's arms and legs were spread out, the water lilies might think it was lots of things diving through them." He looked at Felise. "And how have you been, these last six months?"

"I sleep fourteen hours a day," she said brightly. "Lyle's dying of cancer, probably because he wants to. We all have low self of steam."

"What made you come here today?" asked Evian quietly. "We've been monitoring you closely ever since that night. You never came back here before. In fact according to our schedule you weren't supposed to come here today."

Kokolo looked sharply at Evian. "You're saying this is an anomaly? I don't believe it."

"I'll query Chicago in the window, but I'm pretty sure." Evian looked back at Hollis. "So – why?"

Hollis realized that he was drunk. Good enough for now, but he'd have to get them to fetch another bottle soon.

"Lately," he began. He frowned at Evian, then went on, "Lately I've been dreaming that what happened here, after the part of that night that I could remember, was that – I met myself, finally. And that in fact there isn't anybody else besides me. Like you're all just things I'm imagining because I'm separated from myself now and trying to fill the absence. I – guess I came here today to see if I could meet myself again, somehow, so I can be me and stop being this, this flat roadkill."

"Solipsism," said Felise. "I thought that too, for a while, but it was so obvious that my cat didn't think so, didn't think I was the only thing in the universe, that I decided it wasn't true."

"That's hardly an argument against solipsism!" said Hollis, smiling in spite of himself. "Especially to convince somebody else."

"I could show you the cat," she said.

Kokolo touched his ear and cocked his head. "Lyle's here," he said. "I know that was on the schedule, at least. We should go to the area of measurement."

"We think it was an alien," said Evian as he pushed his chair back and stood up. "Not just a, some creature from another planet, you know, but something that ordinarily exists in more dimensions than the four we live in. Or the five we move in when we travel through time."

Felise had paused to listen to him, and she nodded. "We need more liquor," she said. "Lyle can't drink anymore, but it'd mean a lot to him to see other people still fighting the good fight."

••

One of the two silent men who had stood by the door now opened it and led the way down a carpeted hall to the right; Kokolo and Evian and Scarbee were right behind him, and Hollis and Felise followed more slowly, with the second door-guard coming along last.

The men ahead stopped beside a steel door, and Kokolo pressed his thumb against a tiny glass square above the lever handle.

"This might be disorienting," he said over his shoulder to Hollis, and then he pushed the lever down and opened the door. A puff of chilly air-conditioning ruffled his blond hair.

"It still freaks me," Felise said.

Hollis glimpsed the pool-cue racks mounted on the red-painted walls while the men ahead of him were shuffling into the big room, so he knew what this place was; and when he had stepped through and was standing on the green linoleum floor again for the first time in thirty-one years, he was able to look around at the counters and the bar and the restroom doors in the far wall without any expression of surprise. The lights were all on, and the pinball machines glowed.

"We had the place eminent-domained before you even got outside," said Evian.

The picnic tables and pool tables were still scattered and broken across the floor, and black smears on the linoleum were certainly decades-old blood. The holes in the plaster walls were still raw white against the red paint, though there seemed to be a lighted hallway on the other side now, instead of the alley he remembered. The jagged glass of the front window now had white drywall behind it.

Still dizzy from the stun-gun shock – or freshly drunk – Hollis walked carefully across the littered floor, past the spot at the bar where Felise had always sat when he didn't know her name, and stepped behind the bar to the cash register. He punched in "No Sale," and tore off the receipt. The date on it was June 21, 1975.

On the shelf below the register was the paperback copy of J. P. Donleavy's *The Ginger Man* that Hollis had been reading at the time. He had never bothered to pick up another copy of the book.

Felise had followed Hollis, and now set up one of the fallen barstools and sat down at what used to be her customary place.

Hollis sniffed. The bar, the whole big room, had no smells at all anymore, just a faint chilly whiff of metal.

There was a stack of black bakelite ashtrays on the bar, and he lifted the top one off and pulled the cigarette pack out of his pocket and shook a cigarette onto his lip.

"It's 1975 in here," he called to Scarbee, "check the register tape. Smoking's allowed."

"Five people died here that night," said Evian, who still stood with the others near the door. "Nine survived, though five of them were unresponsively catatonic afterward. And we did try to get responses! The four that survived sane – relatively so – were you, Felise, Lyle, and a four-year-old male child. He died three years ago at the age of thirty-two, in a misadventure during a sadomasochistic orgy."

Felise snickered. "Strangled himself. Can I bum a smoke?"

Hollis slid the pack across to her, then clicked his lighter, but apparently rain had got into it. He picked a Firehouse matchbook out of a box on the shelf and struck one of the matches for her, then held it to his own cigarette.

"Where's Lyle?" he asked as he puffed it alight.

"They're bringing him in," said Evian. "Nurses, IV poles."

"You can't cure him in the future?"

Evian shrugged and widened his eyes. "The past is unalterable! Or we thought so, before you showed up just now where you shouldn't be. Lyle is supposed to die a week from hex. But we've debriefed him very thoroughly, many times, over the years, everything he can give us."

Evian, Kokolo, and Scarbee had begun cautiously stepping out into the room.

"We debriefed *you,*" Evian went on, "with narcohypnosis, right after getting you and your motorcycle back to your apartment, and several times thereafter – you were encouraged to think these interview periods were alcoholic blackouts – and you appeared to remember nothing. But now that you *have* begun to remember what happened, we may as well see if any input from you can manage to prompt something more from Lyle."

"Set up a query transmission to the Chicago window," said Kokolo. "We need to find out for sure that Hollis's visit today isn't an anomaly – the schedule signals aren't always complete, but Chicago can check it against the big chronology. I'm sure he is scheduled to be here – that's probably why we summon Lyle."

"We don't have much bandwidth left in their allotment for hex, it'll have to be a very tight frequency," said Scarbee, edging hesitantly across the linoleum and looking around wide-eyed. Perhaps he had never been in here before. To Hollis he said, "Time may be infinite, but the time-window of our control of the Fermilab accelerator isn't. It uses up a long piece of that duration to negotiate a transmission. They allot us segments of it. And it's not cheap."

"You guys talk pretty freely to strangers," Hollis said.

Kokolo laughed, for the first time. "Like you might tell somebody, call the *L.A. Times?* We know you don't." To Evian he went on, "Check his resonance, then, you can do that with just the carrier-wave link itself, no need for a message. If his resonance is the same as what we've got recorded, we can be pretty sure he hasn't deviated from his plotted time-line."

Evian nodded to Scarbee. "Get a link-station," he said, and Scarbee hurried, with evident relief, out of the preserved pizza parlor.

Hollis stepped through the doorway onto the cement floor of the kitchen. There wasn't much dust on the counter surfaces – higher air-pressure maintained in this whole place, he thought – and the two disks of dough on the work table were clean, though clearly dry as chalk.

Kokolo stepped up on the other side of the counter, and Hollis stopped himself from reflexively reaching for the order pad, which was still right below the telephone.

"We're going to look at your life-line resonance," said Kokolo. "It's a jab in your finger, just enough to hurt."

"You're supposed to die in March of 2008," called Felise cheerfully. "Suicide, while you're on Prozac. At first I thought they said it would be while you had *Kojak* on." She had stepped around behind the bar and was walking toward the kitchen. "I die at forty-eight, but nobody's looked up what year it'll happen in."

"What takes *you* so long?" asked Hollis, turning toward her.

"We both survive it by about thirty years. Subjective years." She smiled at him. "I call that pretty good."

Scarbee had shuffled back into the room, wheeling a cart with something on it that looked like a fax machine. He steered it around the pieces of broken wood.

"We think you survived," said Evian, "weathered the encounter, because you had referents that let you partly roll with the blow; fragment it, deflect it. In your debriefing you talked about Escher prints and Ivan Albright paintings, and William Burroughs, and Ligeti's music. Ionesco, Lovecraft. You were babbling, throwing these things out like cancelled credit cards or phony IDs."

"And I'm still here," said Felise as she lifted one of the hardened dough-disks and let it drop with a clack, "according to these guys, because I was a street girl and a doper. It wasn't a *big* step to get stomped right out of the world." She hiccuped. "Into the cold void between the stars. I wish you still served beer here."

Hollis thought now that he remembered that cold void too. "And Lyle?" said Hollis.

"Lyle was a Christian," Evian said. "Though he stopped being, after that night."

"They figure the four-year-old was abused," said Felise. She rapped the center of one disk with a knuckle, and it broke in a star pattern.

Scarbee had wheeled the device up beside Evian on the other side of the counter. "Give me your hand," he said to Hollis.

Hollis looked at Felise, who nodded. "We've all done it," she said. "It's just a jab, to plug into your nervous system for a second."

"The machine," said Evian, "has a gate in it that's always connected to Fermilab in Chicago in 2015. The time-line of your nervous system is like a long hallway with a mirror at each end – this will tachyonically ring the whole length of it, birth to death, and the resulting, uh, 'note' will show up as a series of lines on a print-out. Interference fringes."

"It's got special cranberry glass rods in it," said Felise helpfully.

"They're colloidal photonic crystals," agreed Scarbee as Hollis reluctantly laid his hand across the order-pickup counter. "Expensive to make. They act as a half-silvered mirror hex, and the machine measures the Cherenkov radiation the tachyons produce as they hit the glass."

He jabbed a needle into Hollis's fingertip. Hollis recoiled and stepped back, blood dripping rapidly from his finger. Felise slid the unbroken dough-disk onto the counter below his hand to catch the drops.

The machine buzzed as a sheet of paper slid out from the front of it, and Scarbee held it up and compared it to a sheet he had brought in.

"They don't match," he said flatly. "His time-line has changed."

"Do I die sooner or later than you thought, now?" asked Hollis, idly drawing a question mark in blood on the dough-disk. But he was aware that his heartbeat had speeded up. The faint metal smell of the room had taken on an oily tang, like ozone.

"Let me see those," snapped Kokolo, stepping over and snatching the papers from Scarbee.

"Can't tell from this," said Scarbee quietly to Hollis, though his eyes were on Kokolo. "Just that it's changed."

"Okay," said Kokolo, dropping the papers, "okay, this seems to be an anomaly. Get Chicago on the line, even if you have to use up all the bandwidth we've got left."

Hollis looked past them at several figures who had entered the room. One was in a wheelchair, and another was pushing a wheeled IV stand beside it.

Hollis squinted at the wasted, bald, skeletal figure in the wheelchair. Presumably it was Don Lyle, but there was apparently nothing left of the cheerful young man Hollis had known.

Scarbee finished pushing a series of buttons on the machine, and paused and then pushed them again. "No connection with Chicago," he said. His voice was hoarse.

Kokolo glanced around quickly with no expression, then reached into his silver jacket and yanked out what looked like a black rubber handlebar-grip.

"You can't leave us hex!" shouted Evian even as Kokolo seemed to squeeze the thing.

Nothing happened. Kokolo stared at his own gripping hand – blood had begun to drip from it – and Evian and Scarbee and Felise stared at him with their mouths open, and Lyle's wheelchair continued to roll forward across the floor.

"Your ejection seat didn't fire," said Felise merrily. "The gate's down – no connection with Chicago at all."

Hollis leaned against the counter, nauseated by the sight of his blood and the taste of the bourbon, and he thought he heard faint voices singing *"Everybody Loves Somebody Sometime"* over the speakers mounted above the take-out counter.

He looked at Felise beside him, but saw curls of color rippling across the room, passing over her face: quick views of the broken pool tables, and the corridors outside the room, and even a night-time parking lot lit by sodium lights – the parking lot that was no longer out front.

His face and hands felt hot.

"Get Lyle out of here!" screamed Kokolo. "It's too similar!"

Then the heavy identity was present again like a subsonic roar and they were all subsumed in its perspective like confetti in a fire.

And rings and spheres appeared in the lamplit air and expanded rapidly, seeming to rush toward Hollis as they grew and rush away from him as they shrank back down to nothing, and more burst into swelling existence everywhere, so that he seemed to be standing in the lanes of some metaphysical freeway.

He had not remembered the noise of it. Tables snapped into pieces and clattered against the walls, masonry broke with booms like cannon shots, and the chilly air whistled around the instantly changing shapes.

The counter he was leaning on crashed backward into the kitchen in a spray of splinters, tumbling him against the base of the oven.

But his frail consciousness was engulfed by the personality that overwhelmed and became his own through its sheer power and age – a person that existed in darkness and infinite emptiness because it had renounced light and everything and everyone that was not itself.

As Hollis's mind imploded it threw up remembered fragments of surrealist paintings, and images from symbolist poems and fairy tales.

This time, though, Hollis's identity wasn't completely assimilated into the thing – he was aware of himself remembering that this had happened before, and so he was able to see it as something separate from himself, though he was sure that his self must at any moment be crushed to oblivion under the infinite psychic weight of the other.

(The cement floor shook under him, and he was remotely aware of screams and crashing.)

This time he was able to perceive that the other was static, unaware of him – rushing through space-time but frozen in one subjective moment of hard-won ruin. And he was aware that it was rushing away from, being powerfully repelled by, something that was its opposite.

Then it was gone and space sprang back into the gap and Hollis was retching and sobbing against the steel foot of the oven, peripherally convinced that the room must be dotted with smoldering fires like a blackened field after a wildfire has passed across it.

A hand was shaking his shoulder, and when he rolled over and looked up at the cracked ceiling he managed to tighten his focus enough to see that someone was bending over him – it was the girl, Felise. Blood was dripping from her nose.

"Out of here," she said. "Lyle too."

Still partly in the perspective of the other, Hollis despised her for her physical presence and the vulgarity of communicating, especially communicating by causing organic membranes to vibrate in air-clotted space – but he struggled to his feet, bracing himself against the oven because he was viscerally aware that he himself was a body standing on a planet that was spinning as it fell through an empty void.

The two of them stumbled out of the kitchen. The bar had been flattened, and they dizzily stepped over the ripped boards and brass strips onto the floor of the dining area. It was difficult for Hollis, and for Felise too, to judge by her hunched posture and short steps, to resist the impulse to crawl on hands and knees.

Evian lay across one of the wrecked picnic tables, his body from the chest down crushed into a new crater in the floor. Scarbee was nowhere to be seen, and Kokolo was standing against the far wall, his lips compressed and his eyes clenched shut.

Lyle's wheelchair was gone, but he lay on his back by the door, and Hollis saw him raise one bloody hand to brush his forehead, chest and shoulders in the sign of the cross before the last of his blood jetted from the stump where his left leg had been.

Hollis's ears were shrilling as if someone had fired a gun in front of his face.

Supporting each other, Hollis and Felise limped out of the pizza parlor into the unlit corridor, and Hollis noticed that she was carrying the link-station machine Scarbee had brought in.

The lights were all out. Part of the wall had been blown in plaster chunks across the corridor, and in the dimness Hollis saw three motionless bodies on the carpet, two of which might have been alive.

"Front door," said Felise hoarsely, stumbling over the pieces of plaster as she led Hollis toward relative brightness ahead.

"My bike," said Hollis. "Away from here."

Felise shook her head. "They'll be out front." She coughed and spat. "Again. Cordoned off again. Stun-guns."

But they both continued toward the gray daylight of the front door, and when Hollis had pushed it open they were both panting as they stepped out onto the breezy pavement, as if they had been holding their breaths.

The parking lot under the overcast sky was empty except for Kokolo's car and Hollis's motorcycle. Cars rushed past on Anaheim Boulevard, but none turned into the lot.

"A bigger area," said Felise, "this time. They'll be closing in any moment."

But Hollis crossed to his motorcycle and swung one leg over it. The key was still in the ignition. He switched it on and tromped on the kick-starter, and the engine sputtered into life. He pushed the kickstand up with his foot and wheeled the bike around to face the street.

"Come on," he called, and Felise, still carrying the steel box, shrugged and walked carefully over to the bike.

"There's no passenger footpegs," she said.

"They fell off," he panted, "a long time ago. Hook your feet over my legs."

She climbed on and folded her legs around him with her feet on the gas tank, clutching him with her hands linked over his chest and the box between his back and her stomach.

He clicked the bike into gear and let the clutch out, and it surged forward into a right turn onto the street.

"How far?" he called over his shoulder as the cold wind ruffled his wet hair.

"Another block or two," she said, and when the bike had roared and bounced through two green-light intersections, she called, "Pull over somewhere."

Hollis downshifted and leaned the bike into a wide supermarket parking lot, and when he had braked it to a halt Felise pushed herself off over the back, hopping on the blacktop to keep her balance while holding the metal box.

"They don't have a cordon," she said. "They're not hex – not here, now." When Hollis got off the bike too and stretched, she laid the box on the frame plate where the seat should have been and pushed buttons on it. "Nothing," she said. "No link to Chicago hex either."

"Maybe the battery's dead," said Hollis.

"The battery is Fermilab in 2015. *That* battery's dead. I better call the New York office." She pulled an ordinary cell phone out of her shirt pocket and tapped in a number. After a moment she said, "Felise, from the field team in Anaheim. I can't raise Chicago. The gate in the link-station seems to be dead." For several seconds she listened, then said, "Right," and closed the phone.

She was frowning. "They say they've lost the link too. But *they* weren't in this locus, for sure." She blinked at Hollis. "No contact here or in New York, not even the carrier-wave signal, no team from the future to move in on the disaster at the Anaheim office – the whole thing's broken down."

For several seconds neither of them spoke, and people parked cars and got out of them to walk toward the supermarket.

Hollis touched his face, and it stung. "Sunburn again," he said.

"Yeah," she said absently, staring at the inert link-station box, "me too."

"The thing," Hollis said, "that passed through – I could perceive more about it this time."

She nodded. "They never were able to change the past, though it's changed now – they had no notes on their charts of anything like this. God knows when you and I die, now. I bet they can't jump at all anymore – I bet we're all left high and dry where we are, now. Some of us in interrupted segments, out of sequence."

She looked around the parking lot as if still hoping a team from the future might come rushing up to debrief them. None did.

"It wasn't...objective," Hollis went on awkwardly. "This time I could tell that I *wasn't* it, and what it let us see was its own chosen situation, not – maybe not – reality. God help us."

"They pushed it too hard," she said sadly, "drilling five-dimensional paths through the solid continuum to jump from point to point of our four-dimensions. Something too heavy rolled over it and it all fell down, like the Tower of Babel. The hour of Babel."

"The thing," he said, "was an opposite of something else, something that's apparently stronger than it, and expelled it."

Felise finally looked at him in exasperation. "Yes, it was a fallen angel, falling at some speed-of-light through space-time, in dimensions that make all this –" She waved at the store and the street and the sky, "– look like figures on a comic-book page. It tore right through our pages, punching one hole that showed up twice in our continuity. Looks like more than one, but it's one."

"Could it have been...*wrong?*" He gave her a twitchy, uncertain smile. "It can't have been *wrong,* can it? After all this time?"

"I don't know. I've spent six months – you've spent thirty-one years! – carrying its perspective." She blinked at him. "What do you suppose the world is really like?"

"I – have no idea."

She shivered. "We thought it was true, didn't we?"

"Or attractive." He climbed back on the idling bike and raised his eyebrows, though it made his forehead sting. "It's still attractive." With his right hand he twisted the throttle, gunning the engine. "Should we get moving?"

"Sure. I think the rain's passed." She carelessly pushed the link-station box off onto the asphalt and climbed on behind him again. "Where to?"

He rubbed his left hand carefully over his face and sighed. Then he laughed weakly. "I think I'd like to see your cat."

•••

When I was working at a place called Firehouse Pizza in the mid-'70s, there was a homeless-looking girl who would come in on slow nights and sit at the far end of the bar, where I would, as-if-by-accident, set trays of half-finished pizzas on their way to the trash cans and sinks in the back room, and eventually she would be gone and the trays would be empty. I don't think she and I ever spoke, beyond her first question about what became of the pizzas left unfinished by customers, and I've wanted to use her in a story ever since.

Firehouse Pizza was exactly how and where I describe it here, and, as in the story, the place where it once stood is now some sort of office building. So for the story I resurrected the old motorcycle I was riding in those days and went back to see what had become of the place, and of that girl. I wound up wrecking the place, but at least I got to talk to her, finally.

–T. P.

75

Parallel Lines

•••

It should have been their birthday today. Well, it was still hers, Caroleen supposed, but with BeeVee gone the whole idea of "birthday" seemed to have gone too. Could she be seventy-three on her own?

Caroleen's right hand had been twitching intermittently since she'd sat up in the living room day-bed five minutes ago, and she lifted the coffee cup with her left hand. The coffee was hot enough but had no taste, and the living room furniture – the coffee table, the now-useless analog TV set with its forlorn rabbit-ears antenna, the rocking chair beside the white-brick fireplace, all bright in the sunlight glaring through the east window at her back – looked like arranged items in some kind of museum diorama; no further motion possible.

But there was still the gravestone to be dealt with, these disorganized nine weeks later. Four hundred and fifty dollars for two square feet of etched granite, and the company in Nevada could not get it straight that Beverly Veronica Erlich and Caroleen Ann Erlich both had the same birth date, though the second date under Caroleen's name was to be left blank for some indeterminate period.

BeeVee's second date had not been left to chance. BeeVee had swallowed all the Darvocets and Vicodins in the house when the pain of her cancer, if it had been cancer, had become more than she could bear.

For a year or so she had always been in some degree of pain – Caroleen remembered how BeeVee had exhaled a fast *whew!* from time to time, and the way her forehead seemed always to be misted with sweat, and her late-acquired habit of repeatedly licking the inner edge of her upper lip. And she had always been shifting her position when she drove, and bracing herself against the floor or the steering wheel. More and more she had come to rely – both of them had come to rely – on poor dumpy Amber, the teenager who lived next door. The girl came over to clean the house and fetch groceries, and seemed grateful for the five dollars an hour, even with BeeVee's generous criticisms of every job Amber did.

But Amber would not be able to deal with the headstone company. Caroleen shifted forward on the day-bed, rocked her head back and forth to make sure she was wearing her reading glasses rather than her bifocals, and flipped open the brown plastic phone book. A short silver pencil was secured by a plastic loop in the book's gutter, and she fumbled it free –

– And her right hand twitched forward, knocking the coffee cup right off the table, and the pencil shook in her spotty old fingers as its point jiggled across the page.

She threw a fearful, guilty glance toward the kitchen in the moment before she remembered that BeeVee was dead; then she allowed herself to relax, and she looked at the squiggle she had drawn across the old addresses and phone numbers.

It was jagged, but recognizably cursive writing, letters:

Ineedyourhelpplease

It was, in fact, recognizably BeeVee's handwriting.

Her hand twitched again, and scrawled the same cramped sequence of letters across the page. She lifted the pencil, postponing all thought in this frozen moment, and after several seconds her hand spasmed once more, no doubt writing the same letters in the air. Her whole body shivered with a feverish chill, and she thought she was going to vomit; she leaned out over the rug, but the queasiness passed.

She was sure that her hand had been writing this message in air ever since she had awakened.

Caroleen didn't think BeeVee had ever before, except with ironic emphasis, said *please* when asking her for something.

She was remotely glad that she was sitting, for her heart thudded alarmingly in her chest and she was dizzy with the enormous thought that BeeVee was not gone, not entirely gone. She gripped the edge of the bed, suddenly afraid of falling and knocking the table over, rolling into the rocking chair. The reek of spilled coffee was strong in her nostrils.

"Okay," she whispered. "Okay!" she said again, louder. The shaking in her hand had subsided, so she flipped to a blank calendar page at the back of the book and scrawled *OKAY* at the top of the page.

Her fingers had begun wiggling again, but she raised her hand as if to wave away a question, hesitant to let the jigging pencil at the waiting page just yet.

Do I want her back, she thought, in any sense? No, not *want,* not *her,* but – in these nine weeks I haven't seemed really to exist anymore, without her paying attention, any sort of attention, to me. These days I'm hardly more than an imaginary friend of Amber next door, a frail conceit soon to be outgrown even by her.

She sighed and lowered her hand to the book. Over her *OKAY* the pencil scribbled,

Iambeevee

"My God," Caroleen whispered, closing her eyes, "you think I need to be told?"

79

Her hand was involuntarily spelling it out again, breaking the pencil lead halfway through but continuing rapidly to the end, and then it went through the motions three more times, just scratching the paper with splintered wood. Finally her hand uncramped.

She threw the pencil on the floor and scrabbled among the orange plastic prescription bottles on the table for a pen. Finding one, she wrote, *What can I do? To help*

She wasn't able to add the final question mark because her hand convulsed away from her again, and wrote,

touseyourbodyinvitemeintoyourbody

and then a moment later,

imsorryforeverythingplease

Caroleen watched as the pen in her hand wrote out the same two lines twice more, then she leaned back and let the pen jiggle in air until this bout too gradually wore off and her hand was limp.

Caroleen blinked tears out of her eyes, trying to believe that they were entirely caused by her already-sore wrist muscles. But – for BeeVee to apologize, to her...! The only apologies BeeVee had ever made while alive were qualified and impatient: *Well I'm* sorry *if...*

Do the dead lose their egotism? wondered Caroleen; their one-time need to limit and dominate earthly households? BeeVee had maintained Caroleen as a sort of extended self, and it had resulted in isolation for the two of them; if in fact they had added up to quite as many as two, during the last years. The twins had a couple of brothers out there somewhere, and at least a couple of nieces, and their mother might even still be alive at ninety-one, but Caroleen knew nothing of any of them. BeeVee had handled all the mail.

Quickly she wrote on the calendar page, *I need to know – do you love me?*

For nearly a full minute she waited, her shoulder muscles stiffening as she held the pen over the page; then her hand flexed and wrote,

yes

Caroleen was gasping and she couldn't see the page through her tears, but she could feel her hand scribbling the word over and over again until this spasm too eventually relaxed.

Why did you have to wait, she thought, until after you had died, to tell me?

But *use your body, invite me into your body.* What would that mean? Would BeeVee take control of it, ever relinquish control?

Do I, thought Caroleen, care, really?

Whatever it might consist of, it would be at least a step closer to the wholeness Caroleen had lost nine weeks ago.

Her hand was twitching again, and she waited until the first couple of scribbles had expended themselves in the air and then touched the pen to the page. The pen wrote,

yesforever

She moved her hand aside, not wanting to spoil that statement with echoes.

When the pen had stilled, Caroleen leaned forward and began writing, *Yes, I'll invite you,* but her hand took over and finished the line with *exhaustedmorelater*

Exhausted? Was it strenuous for ghosts to lean out or in or down this far? Did BeeVee have to brace herself against something to drive the pencil?

But in fact Caroleen was exhausted too – her hand was aching – and she blew her nose on an old Kleenex, her eyes watering afresh in the menthol-and-eucalyptus smell of Bengay, and she lay back across the day-bed and closed her eyes.

••

A sharp knock at the front door jolted her awake, and though her glasses had fallen off and she didn't immediately know whether it was morning or evening, she realized that her fingers were wiggling, and had been for some time.

She lunged forward and with her free hand wedged the pen between her twitching right thumb and forefinger, and then the pen travelled lightly over the calendar page. The scribble was longer than the others, with a pause in the middle, and she had to rotate the book to keep the point on the page until it stopped.

The knock sounded again, but Caroleen called, "Just a minute!" and remained hunched over the little book, waiting for the message to repeat.

It didn't. Apparently she had just barely caught the last echo – perhaps only the end of the last echo.

She couldn't at all make out what she had written – even if she'd had her glasses on, she'd have needed the lamplight too.

"Caroleen?" came a call from out front. It was Amber's voice.

"Coming." Caroleen stood up stiffly and hobbled to the door. When she pulled it open she found herself squinting in noon sunlight filtered through the avocado tree branches.

The girl on the doorstep was wearing sweatpants and a huge T-shirt and blinking behind her gleaming round spectacles. Her brown hair was tied up in a knot on top of her head. "Did I wake you up? I'm sorry." She was panting, as if she had run over here from next door.

Caroleen felt the fresh air, smelling of sun-heated stone and car exhaust, cooling her sweaty scalp. "I'm fine," she said hoarsely. "What is it?" Had she asked the girl to come over today? She couldn't recall doing it, and she was tense with impatience to get back to her pen and book.

"I just," said Amber rapidly, "I liked your sister, well, you know I did really, even though – and I – could I have something of hers, not like valuable, to remember her by? How about her hairbrush?"

"You – want her hairbrush."

"If you don't mind. I just want something –"

"I'll get it, wait here." It would be quicker to give it to her than to propose some other keepsake, and Caroleen had no special attachment to the hairbrush – her own was a duplicate anyway. She and BeeVee had of course had matching everything – toothbrushes, coffee cups, shoes, wristwatches.

When Caroleen had fetched the brush and returned to the front door, Amber took it and went pounding down the walkway, calling "Thanks!" over her shoulder.

Still disoriented from her nap, Caroleen closed the door and made her way back to the bed, where she patted the scattered blankets until she found her glasses and fitted them on.

She sat down and switched on the lamp, and leaned over the phone book page. Turning the book around to follow the newest scrawl, she read,

bancaccounts

getmyhairbrushfromhernow

"Sorry, sorry!" exclaimed Caroleen; then in her own handwriting she wrote, *I'll get it back.*

She waited, wondering why she must get the hairbrush back from Amber. Was it somehow necessary that all of BeeVee's possessions be kept together? Probably at least the ones with voodoo-type identity signatures on them, DNA samples, like hair caught in a brush, dried saliva traces on dentures, Kleenexes in a forgotten waste-basket. But –

Abruptly her chest felt cold and hollow.

But this message had been written down *before* she had given Amber the hairbrush. And Caroleen had been awake only for the last few seconds of the message transmission, which, if it had been like the others, had been repeating for at least a full minute before she woke up.

The message had been addressed to Amber next door, not to her. Amber had read it somehow, and had obediently fetched the hairbrush.

Could all of these messages have been addressed to the girl?

Caroleen remembered wondering whether BeeVee might have needed to brace herself against something in order to communicate from the far side of the grave. Had BeeVee been bracing herself against Caroleen, her still-living twin, in order to talk to Amber? Insignificant *Amber?*

Caroleen was dizzy, but she got to her feet and kicked off her slippers, then padded into the bedroom for a pair of outdoor shoes. She had to carry them back to the living room – the bed in the bedroom had been BeeVee's too, and she didn't want to sit on it in order to pull the shoes on – and on the way, she leaned into the bathroom and grabbed her own hairbrush.

●●

Dressed in one of her old church-attendance skirts, with fresh lipstick, and carrying a big embroidered purse, Caroleen pulled the door closed behind her and began shuffling down the walk. The sky was a very deep blue above the tree branches, and the few clouds were extraordinarily far away overhead, and it occurred to her that she couldn't recall stepping out of the house since BeeVee's funeral. She never drove anymore – Amber was the only one who drove the old

Pontiac these days – and it was Amber who went for groceries, reimbursed with checks that Caroleen wrote out to her, and the box of checks came in the mail, which Amber brought in from the mailbox by the sidewalk. If Caroleen alienated the girl, could she do these things herself? She would probably starve.

Caroleen's hand had begun wriggling as she reached the sidewalk and turned right, toward Amber's parents' house, but she resisted the impulse to pull a pen out of her purse. She's not talking to *me*, she thought, blinking back tears in the sunlight that glittered on the windshields and bumpers of passing cars; she's talking to stupid *Amber*. I won't *eavesdrop*.

Amber's parents had a Spanish-style house at the top of a neatly mowed sloping lawn, and a green canvas awning overhung the big arched window out front. Even shading her eyes with her manageable left hand Caroleen couldn't see anyone in the dimness inside, so she puffed up the widely spaced steps, and while she was catching her breath on the cement apron at the top, the front door swung inward, releasing a puff of cool floor-polish scent.

Amber's young dark-haired mother – Crystal? Christine? – was staring at her curiously. "It's…Caroleen," she said, "right?"

"Yes." Caroleen smiled, feeling old and foolish. "I need to talk to Amber." The mother was looking dubious. "I want to pay her more, and, and see if she'd be interested in balancing our, my, checkbook."

The woman nodded, as if conceding a point. "Well I think that might be good for her." She hesitated, then stepped aside. "Come in and ask her. She's in her room."

Caroleen got a quick impression of a dim living room with clear plastic covers over the furniture, and a bright kitchen with copper pans hung everywhere, and then Amber's mother had knocked on a bedroom door and said, "Amber honey? You've got a visitor," and pushed the door open.

"I'll let you two talk," the woman said, and stepped away toward the living room.

Caroleen stepped into the room. Amber was sitting cross-legged on the pink bedspread, looking up from a cardboard sheet with a rock and a pencil and BeeVee's hairbrush on it. Lacy curtains glowed in the street-side window, and a stack of what appeared to be textbooks stood on an otherwise bare white desk in the opposite corner. The couple of pictures on the walls were pastel blobs. The room smelled like cake.

Caroleen considered what to say. "Can I help?" she asked finally.

Amber, who had been looking wary, brightened and sat up straight. "Shut the door."

When Caroleen had shut it, Amber went on, "You know she's coming back?" She waved at the cardboard in front of her. "She's been talking to me all day."

"I know, child."

Caroleen stepped forward and leaned down to peer at it, and saw that the girl had written the letters of the alphabet in an arc across the cardboard.

"It's one of those things people use to talk to ghosts," Amber explained with evident pride. "I'm using the crystal to point to the letters. Some people are scared of these things, but that's one of the good kind of crystals."

"A Ouija board."

"That's it! She made me dream of one over and over again just before the sun came up, because this is her birthday. Well, yours too I guess. At first I thought it was a hopscotch pattern, but she made me look closer till I got it." She pursed her lips. "I wrote it by reciting the rhyme, and I accidentally did *H* and *I* twice, and left out *J* and *K*." She pulled a sheet of lined paper out from under the board. "But it was only a problem once, I think."

"Can I see? I, uh, want this to work out."

"Yeah, she won't be gone. She'll be in me, did she tell you?" She held out the paper. "I drew in lines to break the words up."

"Yes. She told me." Caroleen slowly reached out to take the paper from her, and then held it up close enough to read the pencilled lines:

I/NEED/YOUR/HELP/PLEASE

Who R U?

I/AM/BEEVEE

How can I help U?

I/NEED/TO/USE/YOUR//BODY/INVITE/ME/IN/TO/YOUR/ BODY IM/SORRY/FOR/EVERY/THING/PLEASE

R U an angel now? Can U grant wishes?

YES

Can U make me beautiful?

YES/FOR/EVER

OK. What do I do?

EXHAUSTED/MORE/LATER

BV? It's after lunch. Are U rested up yet?

YES

Make me beautiful.

GET/MY/HAIRBRUSH/FROM/MY/SISTER

Is that word "hairbrush?"

YES/THEN/YOU/CAN/INVITE/ME/IN/TO/YOU

How will that do it?

WE/WILL/BE/YOU/TOGETHER

+ what will we do?
GET/SLIM/TRAVEL/THE/WORLD
Will we be rich?
YES/I/HAVE/BANC/ACCOUNTS GET/MY/HAIRBRUSH/FROM/
HER/NOW
I got it.
NIGHT/TIME/STAND/OVER/GRAVE/BRUSH/YR/HAIR/INVITE/
ME/IN

"That should be B-A-N-*K*, in that one line," explained Amber helpfully. "And I'll want to borrow your car tonight."

Not trusting herself to speak, Caroleen nodded and handed the paper back to her, wondering if her own face was red or pale. She felt invisible and repudiated. BeeVee could have approached her own twin for this, but her twin was too old; and if she did manage to occupy the body of this girl – a more intimate sort of twinhood! – she would certainly not go on living with Caroleen. And she had eaten all the Vicodins and Darvocets.

Caroleen picked up the rock. It was some sort of quartz crystal.

"When," she began in a croak; she cleared her throat and went on more steadily, "when did you get that second-to-last message? About the bank accounts and the hairbrush?"

"That one? Uh, just a minute before I knocked on your door."

Caroleen nodded, wondering bleakly if BeeVee had even known that she was leaving *her* with carbon copies – multiple, echoing carbon copies – of the messages.

She put the rock back down on the cardboard and picked up the hairbrush. Amber opened her mouth as if to object, then subsided.

There were indeed a number of white hairs tangled in the bristles.

Caroleen tucked the brush into her purse.

"I need that," said Amber quickly, leaning forward across the board. "She says I need it."

"Oh of course, I'm sorry." Caroleen forced what must have been a ghastly smile, and then pulled her own hairbrush instead out of the purse and handed it to the girl. It was identical to BeeVee's, right down to the white hairs.

Amber took it and glanced at it and then laid it on the pillow, out of Caroleen's reach.

"I don't want," said Caroleen, "to interrupt...you two." She sighed, emptying her lungs, and dug the car keys out of her purse. "Here," she said, tossing them onto the bed. "I'll be next door if you...need any help."

"Fine, okay." Amber seemed relieved at the prospect of her leaving.

••

Caroleen was awakened next morning by the pain of her sore right hand flexing, but she rolled over and slept for ten more minutes before the telephone by her head conclusively jarred her out of the monotonous dream that had occupied the last hour or so.

She sat up, wrinkling her nose at the scorched smell from the fireplace and wishing she had a cup of coffee, and still half-seeing the Ouija board she'd been dreaming about.

She picked up the phone, wincing. "Hello?"

"Caroleen," said Amber's voice, "nothing happened at the cemetery last night, and BeeVee isn't answering my questions. She spelled stuff out, but it's not for what I'm writing to her. All she's written so far this morning is – just a sec – she wrote, uh, 'You win – you'll do – We've always been a team, right –' Is she talking to you?"

Caroleen glanced toward the fireplace, where last night she had burned – or charred, at least – BeeVee's toothbrush, razor, dentures, curlers, and several other things, including the hairbrush. And today she would call the headstone company and cancel the order. BeeVee ought not to have an easily locatable grave.

"Me?" Caroleen made a painful fist of her right hand. "Why would she talk to me?"

"You're her twin sister, she might be –"

"BeeVee is dead, Amber, she died nine weeks ago."

"But she's coming back, she's going to make me beautiful! She said –"

"She can't do anything, child. We're better off without her."

Amber was talking then, protesting, but Caroleen's thoughts were of the brothers she couldn't even picture anymore, the nieces she'd never met and who probably had children of their own somewhere, and her mother who was almost certainly dead by now. And there was everybody else, too, and not a lot of time.

Caroleen was resolved to learn to write with her left hand, and, even though it would hurt, she hoped her right hand would go on and on writing uselessly in air.

At last she stood up, still holding the phone, and she interrupted Amber: "Could you bring back my car keys? I've got some errands."

• • •

Like a lot of people of my generation, my wife and I spent a year – 2007, in our case – visiting elderly parents in "assisted living homes," the kind of places where the dining room has tables but no chairs because all the diners will arrive in wheelchairs, and there are banners advancing sentiments like,

"Sunsets are as beautiful as sunrises," which can come to seem bitterly ironic.

In one of these places I was standing against the wall of a corridor so that two extremely elderly ladies could be wheeled past one another — and as they crossed, one of them croaked at the other, "Bitch!"

It occurred to me that a story about conflicts between two very old people would be fun — and of course I had to put a ghost in it.

And I teach one class a week at the Orange County High School of the Arts — the other end of the age spectrum! — and the school building used to be a nineteenth-century church. My classroom is the basement catacombs, and one afternoon when I had given the students an assignment and they had all dispersed throughout the church to write, I found two of the girls huddled over a box that they had converted into a makeshift Ouija board, using a crystal for a planchette. When I said, "What the hell!" one of them quickly explained, "It's okay, Mr. Powers, it's one of the good kind of crystals!"

Oh. Well then.

So I had to give Amber their Ouija board.

—T. P.

A JOURNEY OF ONLY TWO PACES

•••

She had ordered steak tartare and Hennessy XO brandy, which would, he reflected, look extravagant when he submitted his expenses to the court. And God knew what parking would cost here.

He took another frugal sip of his beer and said, trying not to sound sour, "I could have mailed you a check."

They were at one of the glass-topped tables on the outdoor veranda at the Beverly Wilshire Hotel, just a couple of feet above the sidewalk beyond the railing, looking out from under the table's umbrella down the sunlit lanes of Rodeo Drive. The diesel-scented air was hot even in the shade.

"But you were his old friend," she said. "He always told me that you're entertaining." She smiled at him expectantly.

She had been a widow for about ten years, Kohler recalled – and she must have married young. In her sunglasses and broad Panama hat she only seemed to be about twenty now.

Kohler, though, felt far older than his thirty-five years.

"He was easily entertained, Mrs. Halloway," he said slowly. "I'm pretty...lackluster, really." A young man on the other side of the railing overheard him and glanced his way in amusement as he strode past on the sidewalk.

93

"Call me Campion. But a dealer in rare books must have some fascinating stories."

Her full name was Elizabeth St. Campion Halloway. She signed her paintings "Campion." Kohler had looked her up online before driving out here to deliver the thousand dollars, and had decided that all her artwork was morbid and clumsy.

"He found you attractive," she went on, tapping the ash off her cigarette into the scraped remains of her steak tartare. He noticed that the filter was smeared with her red lipstick. "Did he ever tell you?"

"Really. No." For all Kohler knew, Jack Ranald might have been gay. The two of them had only got together about once a year since college, and then only when Kohler had already begged off on two or three email invitations. Kohler's wife had always thought Jack was inwardly mocking her – *He forgets me when he's not looking right at me,* she'd said – and she wouldn't have been pleased with these involvements in the dead man's estate.

Kohler's wife had looked nothing like Campion.

Campion was staring at him now over the coal of her cigarette – he couldn't see her eyes behind the dark lenses, but her pale, narrow face swung carefully down and left and right. "I can already see him in you. You have the Letters Testamentary?"

"Uh." The shift in conversational gear left him momentarily blank. "Oh, yes – would you like to see them? and I'll want a receipt –"

"Not the one from the court clerk. The one Jack arranged."

Kohler bent down to get his black vinyl briefcase, and he pushed his chair back from the table to unzip it on his lap. Inside were all the records of terminating the water and electric utilities at the house Jack had owned in Echo Park and paying off Jack's credit cards, and, in a manila envelope along with the death certificate – which discreetly didn't mention suicide – the letters he had been given by the probate court.

One of them was the apparently standard sort, signed by the clerk and the deputy clerk, but the other had been prepared by Jack himself.

Kohler tugged that one out and leaned forward to hand it across the table to Campion, and while she bent her head over it he mentally recalled its phrases: *...having been appointed and qualified as enactor of the will of John Carpenter Ranald, departed, who expired on or about 28 February 2009, Arthur Lewis Kohler is hereby authorized to function as enactor and to consummate possession...* In effect it was a suicide note. It had been signed in advance by Jack, and Kohler had recently been required to sign it too.

"Kabbalah," she said, without looking up, and for a moment Kohler thought he had somehow put one of his own business invoices into the briefcase by mistake and handed it to her. She looked up and smiled at him. "Are you afraid to get drunk with me? I'm sure one beer won't release any pent-up emotions, you can safely finish it. What *is* the most valuable book you have in stock?"

Kohler was frowning, but he went along with her change of subject. Jack must have told her what sort of books he specialized in.

"I guess that would be a manuscript codex of a thing called the *Gallei Razayya,* written in about 1550. It, uh, differs from the copy at Oxford." He shrugged. "I've got it priced high – it'll probably just go to my," he hesitated, then sighed and completed the habitual sentence, "my heirs."

"Rhymes with prayers, and you don't have any, do you? Heirs? Anymore? I was so sorry to hear about that."

Kohler stared at her, wondering if he wanted to make the effort of taking offense at her flippancy.

"No," he said instead, carefully.

"But it's about transmigration of souls, isn't it? Your codex book? Maybe you could...bequeath it to yourself."

She pushed her own chair back and stood up, brushing out her white linen skirt. "Have you tried to find the apartment building he owned in Silver Lake?"

Kohler began hastily to zip up his briefcase, and he was about to ask her how she knew about the manuscript when he remembered that she was still holding the peculiar Letter Testamentary.

"Uh...?" he said, reaching for it.

"I'll keep it for a while," she said gaily, tucking it into her purse. "I bet you couldn't find the place."

"That's true." He lowered his hand and finished zipping the case; the letter signed by the clerks was the legally important one. "I need to get the building assessed for the inventory of the estate. The address on the tax records seems to be wrong." Finally he asked, "You...know a lot about Kabbalah?"

"I can take you there. The address is wrong, as you say. Do you like cats? Jack told me about your book, your *codex.*"

Kohler got to his feet and drank off half of the remaining beer in his glass. It wasn't very cold by this time. Jack had always wanted to hear about Kohler's business – Kohler must have acquired the manuscript shortly before they had last met for dinner, and told Jack about it.

"Sure," he said distractedly. She raised one penciled eyebrow, and he added, "I like cats fine."

"I'll drive," she said. "I have no head for directions, I couldn't guide you." She started toward the steps down to the Wilshire Boulevard sidewalk, then turned back and frowned at his briefcase. "You've followed all the directions he left in his will?"

Kohler guessed what she was thinking of. "The urn is in the trunk of my car," he said.

"You can drive. Your car is smaller, better for the tight turns."

Kohler followed her down out of the hotel's shadow onto the glaring Wilshire sidewalk, wondering how she knew what sort of car he drove, and when he had agreed to go right now to look at the apartment building.

••

She directed him east to the Hollywood freeway and then up into the hills above the Silver Lake Reservoir. The roads were narrow and twisting and overhung with carob and jacaranda trees.

Eventually, after Kohler had lost all sense of direction, Campion said, "Turn left at that street there."

"That? That's a driveway," Kohler objected, braking to a halt.

"It's the street," she said. "Well, lane. Alley. Anyway, it's where the apartment building is. Where are you living these days?"

In an apartment building, Kohler thought, probably not as nice as the one we're trying to find here. The old house was just too unbearably familiar. "Culver City."

"Did you like him? Jack?"

Kohler turned the wheel sharply and then steered by inches up onto the narrow strip of pavement, which curled away out of sight to the right behind a hedge of white-blooming oleander only a few yards ahead. Dry palm-fronds scattered across the cracked asphalt crunched under the tires. The needle of the temperature gauge was still comfortably on the left side of the dial, but he kept an eye on it.

"I liked him well enough," he said, squinting through the alternating sun-glare and palm-trunk shadows on the windshield. He exhaled.

"Actually I didn't, no. I liked him in college, but after his father died, he – he just wasn't the same guy anymore."

"It was a shock," she said, nodding. "A trauma. He had heartworms."

Kohler just shook his head. "And Jack was sick, he said. What was wrong with him?"

She shrugged. "What does it matter? Something he didn't want to wait for. But –" And then she sang, "We're young and health*y*, so let's be *bold."* She giggled. "Do you remember that song?"

"No."

"No, it would have been before your time."

The steep little road did seem to be something more than a driveway – Kohler kept the Saturn to about five miles an hour, and they slowly rumbled past several old Spanish-style houses with white stucco walls and red roof-tiles and tiny garages with green-painted doors, the whole landscape as apparently empty of people as a street in a de Chirico painting. Campion had lit another cigarette, and Kohler cranked down the driver's-side window, and even though it was hot he was grateful for the sage and honeysuckle breeze.

"It's on the right," she said, tapping the windshield with a fingernail. "The arch there leads into the parking court."

Kohler steered in through the chipped white arch between tall trees, and he was surprised to see five or six cars parked in the unpaved yard and a big Honda Gold Wing motorcycle leaning on its stand up by the porch, in the shade of a vast lantana bush that crawled up the side of the two-story old building.

"Tenants?" he said, rocking the Saturn into a gap beside a battered old Volkswagen. "I hope…what's-his-name, the guy who inherited the place, wants to keep it running." A haze of dust raised by their passage across the yard swirled over the car.

"Mister Bump. He will, he lives here." She pointed at the motorcycle. "Jack's bike – running boards, a windshield, stereo, passenger seat – it's as if his RV had pups."

Kohler hadn't turned off the engine. "I could do this through the mail, if I could get a valid address."

"They get mail here, sort of informally. Somebody will tell you how to address it." She had opened her door and was stepping out onto the dry dirt, so he sighed and twisted the ignition key back and pulled it out. Now he could hear a violin playing behind one of the upstairs balconies – some intricate phrase from *Scheherazade,* rendered with such gliding expertise that he thought it must be a recording.

With the wall around it, and the still air under the old pepper trees, this compound seemed disconnected from the surrounding streets and freeways of Los Angeles.

"These were Jack's friends," Campion said. "Bring the urn."

Kohler was already sweating in the harsh sunlight, but he walked to the trunk and bent down to open it. He lifted out the heavy cardboard box and slammed the trunk shut.

"Jack is who we all have in common," said Campion, smiling and taking his free arm.

She led Kohler across the yard and up the worn stone steps to the porch, and the French doors stood open onto a dim, high-ceilinged lobby.

The air was cooler inside, and Kohler could hear an air-conditioner rattling away somewhere behind the painted screens and tapestries and potted plants that hid the walls. Narrow beams of sunlight slanted in and gleamed on the polished wooden floor.

Then Kohler noticed the cats. First two on an old Victorian sofa, then several more between vases on high shelves, and after a moment he decided that there must be at least a dozen cats in the room, lazily staring at the newcomers from heavy-lidded topaz eyes.

The cats were all identical – long-haired orange and white creatures with long fluffy tails.

"Campion!"

A tanned young man in a Polo shirt and khaki shorts had walked into the lobby through the French doors on the far side, and Kohler glimpsed an atrium behind him – huge shiny green leaves and orchid blossoms motionless in the still air.

"You *bitch*," the man said cheerfully, "did you lose your phone? Couldn't at least *honk* while you were driving up? 'Tis just like a summer birdcage in a garden.'"

"Mr. Bump," said Campion, "I've brought James Kohler for the, the *wake.*"

"No," said Kohler hastily, "I can't stay –"

"Can I call you Jimmy?" interrupted Mr. Bump. He held out his hand. "Mentally I'm spelling it J-I-M-I, like Hendrix."

Kohler shook the man's brown hand, then after several seconds flexed his own hand to separate them.

"No time to go a-waking, eh?" said Mr. Bump with a smile.

"I'm afraid not. I'll just –"

"Is that Jack?"

Kohler blinked, then realized that the man must be referring to the box he carried in his left hand.

"Oh. Yes."

"Let's walk him out to the atrium, shall we? We can disperse his ashes in the garden there."

Over Mr. Bump's shoulder, one of the orange cats on a high shelf flattened its ears.

"I'm supposed to –" Kohler paused to take a breath before explaining Jack Ranald's eccentric instructions. "I'm supposed to give him – his ashes – to somebody who quotes a certain poem to me. And I think it would be illegal to…pour out the ashes in a, a residence."

Behind him Campion laughed. "It's not a *poem.*"

"Jimi isn't literary, is all," said Mr. Bump to her reprovingly. He crouched to pick up a kitten that seemed to be an exact miniature copy of all the other cats.

I'm a rare-books dealer! thought Kohler, but he just turned to her and said, "What is it?"

"I quoted a bit of it just now," said Mr. Bump, holding the kitten now and stroking it. "'Tis just like a summer birdcage in a garden; the birds that are without despair to get in, and the birds that are within despair and are in a consumption for fear they shall never get out.'"

Kohler nodded – that was it. The will had specified the phrase, *Consumption for fear they shall never get out,* and he had assumed it was a line of anapestic quatrameter.

"What's it from?" he asked, setting the box on a table and lifting out of it the black ceramic urn.

"A play," said Campion, taking his free arm again, apparently in anticipation of walking out to the atrium. "Webster's *The White Devil.*"

"It's a filthy play," put in Mr. Bump.

The cats were bounding down from their perches and scurrying out the far doors into the atrium, their tails waving like a field of orange ferns in a wind.

The three people followed the cats out into the small, tiled courtyard that lay below second-floor balconies on all four sides. The atrium was crowded with tropical-looking plants, and leafy branches and vines hid some corners of the balconies – but Kohler noted uneasily that more than a dozen young men and women were leaning on the iron railings and silently looking down on them. The air smelled of jasmine and cat-boxes.

"The character who says the birdcage business," remarked Campion, "rises from the dead, at the end."

"And then gets killed again," noted Mr. Bump.

Campion shrugged. "Still." She looked up at the audience on the balconies. "Jack's back!" she called. "This nice man has been kind enough to carry him."

The men and women on the balconies all began snapping their fingers, apparently by way of applause. Kohler was nervously tempted to bow.

They didn't stop, and the shrill clacking began to take on a choppy rhythm.

The cats had all sat down in a ring in the center of the atrium floor – no, Kohler saw, it wasn't a ring, it was a triangle, and then he saw that they were all sitting on three lines of red tile set into the pavement. The space inside the triangle was empty.

Campion had stepped away to close the French doors to the lobby, and Mr. Bump leaned close to Kohler and spoke loudly to be heard over the shaking rattle from above. "This is the last part of your duty as executor," he said. The kitten he was holding seemed to have gone to sleep, in spite of the noise.

"It's not the last, by any means," said Kohler, who was sweating again. "There's the taxes, and selling the house, and – and I don't think this *is* part of my duties." He squinted up at the finger-snapping people – they were all dressed in slacks and shirts that were black or white, and the faces he could make out were expressionless. *Something's happening here,* he thought, *and you don't know what it is.* The sweat was suddenly cold on his forehead, and he pushed the urn into Mr. Bump's hands.

"I have to leave," Kohler said, turning back toward the lobby. "Now."

Campion stood in front of the closed doors, and she was pointing a small black automatic pistol at him – it looked like .22 or .25 caliber. "It was so kind of you to come!" she cried merrily. "And you are very nice!"

Kohler was peripherally aware that what she had said was a quote from something, but all his attention was focused on the gun muzzle. Campion's finger was inside the trigger guard. He stopped moving, then slowly extended his empty hands out to the side, his fingers twitching in time to his heartbeat.

Mr. Bump shook his head and smiled ruefully at Kohler. "Campion is so *theatrical!* We just, we'd be very grateful if you'd participate in a – memorial service."

The people on the balconies must have been able to see the situation, but the counterpoint racket never faltered – clearly there would be no help from them, whoever they were. "Then," said Kohler hoarsely, "I can go?"

"You might very well prefer to stay," said Campion. "It's a leisurely life."

Stay? Kohler thought.

"What," he asked, "do I do?"

"You were his closest friend," said Mr. Bump, "so you should –"

"I hardly knew him! Since college, at least. Maybe once or twice a year –"

"You're who he nominated. You should step over the cats, into the open space there, and after everybody has recited Jack's Letter Testamentary, you simply break the urn. At your feet."

Mr. Bump pressed the urn into Kohler's right hand, and Kohler closed his fingers around the glassy neck of it.

"And then I – can leave."

Campion nodded brightly. "Yours will be a journey only of two paces into view of the stars again," she said.

Kohler recognized what she had said as lines from a Walter de la Mare poem, and he recalled how the sentence in the poem ended – *but you will not make it.*

And belatedly he recognized what she had said a few moments ago: *It was so kind of you to come! And you are very nice!* – that was from Lewis Carroll's "The Walrus and the Carpenter," spoken by the Walrus just before he and the Carpenter began devouring the gullible Oysters.

Kohler was grasping the urn in both hands, and now he had to force his arms not to shake in time to the percussive rhythm of all the rattling hands. He glanced at Campion, but she was still holding the gun pointed directly at the middle of him.

"You really should have had more to drink," she called.

God only knew who these people were, or what weird ritual this was, and Kohler was considering causing some kind of diversion and just diving over some plants and rolling through one of the ground-floor French doors, and then just running. Out of this building, over the wall, and away.

It seemed unrealistic.

He obediently stepped over the cats into the clear triangle of pavement.

"Now wait till they've recited it all," said Mr. Bump loudly.

With her free hand Campion dug the peculiar Letter Testamentary out of her purse and flapped it in the still air to unfold it.

And then a young woman on one of the balconies whispered, "*Having...*" and a man on a balcony on the other side of the atrium whispered, "*...been...*" and another followed with "*...appointed...*"

The hoarse whispers undercut the shrill finger-snapping and echoed clearly around the walled space. They were reciting the text of Jack's letter, and each was enunciating only one word of it, letting a pause fall between each word.

The glassy bulge of the urn was slippery in Kohler's sweating hands, and he assembled some of the disjointed phrases in his mind: *enactor of the will of John Carpenter Ranald...Arthur Lewis Kohler...to consummate possession...*

And he recognized this technique – in first century Kabbalistic mysticism, certain truths could be spoken only in whispers, and the writing of certain magical texts required that a different scribe write each separate word.

As clearly as if she were speaking now, Campion's words at lunch came back to him: *But it's about transmigration of souls, isn't it?* and *I can already see him in you.*

And he recalled saying, *after his father died, he just wasn't the same guy anymore.*

Jack Ranald had been executor of his father's will.

"To," whispered one of the black-or-white-clad people on the balconies. *"Consummate,"* whispered another. *"Possession,"* breathed one more, and then they stopped, and the finger-snapping stopped too. The silence that followed seemed to spring up from the paving stones, and the cats sitting in a triangle around Kohler shifted in place.

Mr. Bump nodded to Kohler and raised the kitten in both hands.

"Where do you want to go, from here?" whispered Campion. "Is there anything *you* want to wait for?"

Kohler sighed, a long exhalation that relaxed all his muscles and seemed to empty him. Go? he thought. Back to my studio apartment in Culver City...Wait for? No. I *could* do this – I *could* stay here, hidden from everything, even from myself, it seems.

He could hear the cats around the triangle purring. It's a leisurely life, Campion had said.

"What have you got to lose?" whispered Campion.

Lose? he thought. Nothing – nothing but memories I don't seem to have room for anymore.

And he remembered again what his wife had said about Jack – *He forgets me when he's not looking right at me.* Kohler couldn't look at her anymore –

– but to do this, whatever it was, would pretty clearly be to join Jack.

Kohler took a deep breath, and he felt as if he were stepping back out of a warm doorway, back into the useless tensions of a cold night.

And he flung the urn as hard as he could straight up. Everyone's eyes followed it, and Kohler stepped out of the triangle and, in a sudden moment of inspiration, picked up one of the cats and leaned forward to set it down in the clear triangular patch before hurrying toward a door away from Campion.

The urn shattered on the pavement behind him with a noise like a gunshot as Kohler was grabbing the doorknob, but two sounds stopped him – the cat yowled two syllables and, in perfect synchronization, a voice in his head said, in anguish, *Jimmy.*

It was Jack's voice. Even the cat's cry had seemed to be Jack's voice.

Helplessly Kohler let go of the doorknob and turned around.

The rest of the cats had scattered. Campion had hurried into the triangular space, the gun falling from her fingers and skittering across the paving stones, and she was cradling the cat Kohler had put there. Mr. Bump had let the kitten jump down from his arms now and was just staring open-mouthed, and the people on the balconies were leaning forward and whispering in agitation – but their whispers now weren't audible.

"Jack!" Campion said hitchingly through tears, "Jack, darling, what has he done, what has he done?"

The cat was staring over Campion's shoulder directly at Kohler, and

Kohler shivered at its intense amber glare.

But he nodded and said softly, "So long, Jack." Then he recalled that it was probably Jack's father, and looked away.

He took two steps forward across the tiles and picked up the little automatic pistol that Campion had dropped. There seemed to be no reason now not to leave by the way he'd come in.

Mr. Bump was shaking his head in evident amazement. "It was supposed to be you," he said, standing well back as he held the lobby door open, "into the kitten, to make room for Jack. That cat's already got somebody – I don't know how that'll work out." He stepped quickly to keep up with Kohler's stride across the dim lobby toward the front doors. "No use, anyway, they can't even write. Just not enough brain in their heads!" He laughed nervously, watching the gun in Kohler's hand. "You're – actually going to *leave* then?"

At the front doors, with his hand on one of the old iron handles, Kohler stopped. "I don't think anybody would want me to stay."

Mr. Bump shrugged. "I think Campion likes you. Likes *you*, I mean, too." He smiled. "'Despair to get in,' and I think you've paid the entry fee. Stay for dinner, at least? I'm making a huge cioppino, plenty for everybody, even the cats."

Kohler found that he was not sure enough about what had happened, not *quite* sure enough, to make the impossible denunciations that he wanted to make. It might help to read some of the books in his stock, but at this moment he was resolved never to open one again except to catalogue it.

So "Give Jack mine," was all he said, as he pulled the door open; and then he hurried down the steps into the sunlight, reaching into his pocket for his car keys and bleakly eyeing the lane that would lead him back down to the old, old, terribly familiar freeway.

•••

Los Angeles is my favorite city. Anybody can fall in love with San Francisco or New Orleans in ten minutes, but Los Angeles is more circumspect. There are lots of odd, secluded spots down in the canyons or up on the hilltops between the freeways – domed temples from the 1920s that still host some furtive sort of worship, eccentric gardens that stretch implausible distances, nearly inaccessible old apartment buildings whose tenants seem to be covertly united in some secret cause. The odd place in this story was based on one such apartment building where my wife and I one day found the street-side lobby door unlocked.

–T. P.

A Time to Cast Away Stones

•••

Sometimes it's one of the supporting-role characters that stays with you. In the lurid sagas of Jack Kerouac and Ken Kesey, the tangential figure of Neal Cassady is ultimately the most memorable for me. And in the lives of Byron and Shelley, and then fifty years later the lives of the Rossetti family and the Pre-Raphaelites, it's the enduring figure of Edward John Trelawny that lingers most in my mind.

Trelawny figured peripherally in my 1989 novel The Stress of Her Regard, *and, as an old man, in my newest novel, the title of which has as of this writing not yet been decided on. But really the most important adventure of Trelawny's life took place in the years between the times those books cover – specifically in 1824 and 1825, in Greece.*

Joe Stefko at Charnel House was the original publisher of The Stress of Her Regard, *and for the twentieth anniversary of the press he asked me if I could write something further involving Shelley and Byron; and it turned out that Trelawny was the most intriguing person in the crowd.*

In order to write this story I read Trelawny's autobiography, Adventures of a Younger Son, *which for more than a hundred years was taken as factual and has only recently been revealed to be entirely a romantic fiction; and the 1940 biography* Trelawny *by Margaret Armstrong, written before Trelawny's deception was discovered; and the more recent and accurate biographies, William St. Clair's* Trelawny, The Incurable Romancer, *and David Crane's* Lord Byron's Jackal.

Somebody once said that you become what you pretend to be, and Trelawny had always pretended to be a romantic character out of one of Byron's swashbuckling tales. In the end I admire him.

–*T. P.*

•••

I

May 1825

"Though here no more Apollo haunts his Grot,
And thou, the Muses' seat, art now their grave,
Some gentle Spirit still pervades the spot,
Sighs in the gale, keeps silence in the Cave..."

– Lord Byron

"Oh, thou Parnassus!"

– from *Childe Harold's Pilgrimage,*
Canto I, LXII

Somewhere ahead in the windy darkness lay the village of Tithorea, and south of that the pass through the foothills to the crossroads where, according to legend, Oedipus killed his father. Trelawny and his young wife would reach it at dawn, and then ride east, toward Athens, directly away from Delphi and Mount Parnassus.

But it was only midnight now, and they were still in the Velitza Gorge below Parnassus, guiding their horses down the pebbly dry bed of the Kakoreme by the intermittent moonlight. It was half an hour since they had left behind the smells of tobacco smoke and roasted pigeon as they had skirted wide through the oaks around the silent tents of Ghouras's palikars at the Chapel of St. George, and now the night wind in Trelawny's face smelled only of sage and clay, but he still listened for the sound of pursuing hoofbeats...or for stones clattering or grinding, or women's voices singing atonally out in the night.

The only sound now, though, was the homely thump and knock of the horses' hooves. He glanced to his right at Tersitza – huddled in her shaggy sheepskin cape, she seemed like a child rocking in the saddle, and Trelawny recalled Byron's words:

And then – that little girl, your warlord's sister? – she'll be their prey, and change to one of them – supposing that you care about the child.

Byron had said it only three months after dying in Missolonghi last year, and at the time it had not been a particularly important point – but now Tersitza was Trelawny's wife, and Trelawny was determined to get her free of her brother's ambitions...the ambitions which until a few months ago had been Trelawny's too. A man had to protect his wife.

A great man?

The intruding thought was so strong that Trelawny almost glanced around at the shadows among the twisted olive trees here to see who had whispered it; but he kept his eyes on Tersitza. He wished she would glance over at him, show him that she was still there, that she still had a face.

Percy Shelley hadn't protected his wife – his first wife, at least, Harriet. He had abandoned her in England and run off to Switzerland to wed Mary Godwin, and Harriet had in fact died a year or two later, in the Serpentine River in Hyde Park. Shelley had been a great man, though, one of the immortal poets – a true king of Parnassus! – and such men couldn't be bound by pedestrian moralities out of old holy books. Trelawny had been proud to call Shelley his friend, and had eventually overseen the poet's cremation and burial. Shelley had been a braver man than Byron, who for all his manly posturing and licentious ways had proven to be a willing prisoner of...convention, propriety, human connections.

A warm wind had sprung up now at their backs, tossing the loose ends of Trelawny's turban across his bearded face, and he smelled jasmine. *All the kingdoms of the world, and the glory of them,* he thought. I am even now literally turning my back on them.

With the thought, he was instantly tempted to rein in the horses and retrace their course. The British adventurer, Major Francis Bacon, would be returning here, ideally within a few weeks, and if Bacon kept his promise he would be bringing with him the talisman that would... would let Trelawny do what Byron had advised.

But he bitterly recognized the dishonesty of his own rationalization. Major Bacon would probably not be able to make his way back here before Midsummer's Eve, and after that it would almost certainly be too late. And – and Trelawny had told Tersitza that their expedition tonight was to rescue her brother, the *klepht* warlord Odysseus Androutses, from his captivity in the Venetian Tower at the Acropolis in Athens. Odysseus had been imprisoned there two weeks ago by his one-time lieutenant, Ghouras, whose palikars were already camped in several places right here in the Velitza Gorge. Trelawny knew that Ghouras meant soon to blockade the mountain entirely, and that tonight might be the last chance he and Tersitza would have to escape.

He had no choice but to turn his back on the mountain, and on the glamorous damnation it offered.

Not for the first time, he forced down the forlorn wish that Byron had never spoken to him after dying in Missolonghi.

••

A year ago, in April of 1824, Edward Trelawny had ridden west from Athens toward Missolonghi with a troop of armed palikars, eager to show Lord Byron that an alliance with certain maligned old forces really *was* possible, and would be the best way to free Greece from the Turks. Previously, especially on the boat over from Italy, Byron had laughed at Trelawny's aspirations – but shortly after their arrival in Greece, Trelawny had left the dissolute lord's luxurious quarters in Cephalonia and struck out on his own across the war-ravaged Greek countryside, and had eventually found the *klepht*, the Greek warlord, who knew something of the ancient secret ways to summon such help – and to virtually make gods of the humans who established the contact.

As Trelawny had furtively guided his band of palikars westward through the chilly mountain passes above the Gulf of Corinth, hidden by the crags and pines from the Turkish cavalry on the slopes below, he had rehearsed what he would say to Byron when they reached Missolonghi: *The* klepht *Odysseus Androutses and I have already paid the toll, in rivers of Turkish blood on the island of Euboaea, and in blood of our own drawn by the metal that's lighter than wood – we have our own army, and our headquarters are on Mount Parnassus itself, the very home of the Muses! It's all true – join us, take your rightful place on Parnassus in the soon-to-be-immortal flesh!*

Byron wasn't nearly the poet that Shelley had been, in Trelawny's estimation, but surely any poet would have been flattered by the Parnassus allusion, Parnassus being the home of the goddesses called the Muses in classical Greek myths, and sacred to poetry and music. Trelawny would not remind Byron that Mount Parnassus was also reputed to be the site where Deucalion and Pyrrha landed their ark, after the great flood, and repopulated the world by throwing over their shoulders stones that then grew up into human form.

And Trelawny would not mention, not right away, his hope that Byron, who had once had dealings with these powers himself before foolishly renouncing them, would act in the role the Arabs called *rafiq:* a recognized escort, a maker of introductions that otherwise might be dangerous.

Trelawny had imagined that Byron would finally lose his skeptical smirk, and admit that Trelawny had preceded him in glory – and that the lord would gladly agree to serve as *rafiq* to the powers which Trelawny and Odysseus Androutsos hoped to summon and join – but on the bank of the Evvenus River, still a day's ride west of the mudbank seacoast town of Missolonghi, Trelawny's band had passed a disordered group of palikars fleeing east, and when Trelawny had asked one of the haggard soldiers for news, he learned that Lord Byron had died five days earlier.

Damn the man!

Byron had died still intolerably imagining that Trelawny was a fraud – *If we could make Edward tell the truth and wash his hands we will make a gentleman of him yet,* Byron had more than once remarked to their mutual friends in Italy – and that all Trelawny's reminiscences about having captured countless ships on the Indian Ocean as second-in-command to the noble privateer de Ruyters, and marrying the beautiful Arab princess Zela, were fantasies born of nothing but his imagination. Trelawny had always been sourly aware of Byron's amiable skepticism.

••

His horse snickered and tossed its head in the moonlight, and Trelawny

glanced at Tersitza – who still swayed in the saddle of the horse plod-
ding along beside his, still silently wrapped in her shaggy cape – and
then he peered fearfully back at the sky-blotting bulk of Mount Parnassus. It hardly seemed to have receded into the distance at all since they
had left. If anything, it seemed closer.

••

Only to himself, and only sometimes, could Edward Trelawny admit
that in fact he *had* concocted all the tales of his previous history – he
had *not* actually deserted the British Navy at the age of sixteen to
become a corsair and marry a princess who died tragically, but had
instead continued as an anonymous midshipman and been routinely
discharged from the Navy in Portsmouth at twenty, with not even the
half-pay a lieutenant would get. A sordid marriage had followed a year
later, and after the birth of two daughters his wife had eloped with
a captain of the Prince of Wales's Regiment. Trelawny, then twenty-
four, had vowed to challenge the man to a duel, though nothing had
come of it.

But his stories had become so real to him, as he had repeated them in
ever-more-colorful detail to Shelley and Mary and the rest of the expa-
triate British circle in Pisa in the early months of 1822, that Trelawny's
memory served them up to his recall far more vividly than it did the
tawdry, humiliating details of the actual events.

And now he *was* living the sort of life he had only imagined – only
foreseen! – back in Italy. He habitually dressed now in Suliote cos-
tume, the red and gold vest and the sheepskin *capote*, with pistols
and a sword in his sash, and he was second-in-command to Odysseus
Androutses, a real brigand chief, and together they had killed dozens

of Ali Pasha's Turkish soldiers on the occupied island of Euboaea.

••

But the memories of ambushing Turks and burning their villages on Euboaea brought up bile to the back of his throat now, and made him want to goad the horses into a foolhardy gallop through the patchy moonlight. It wasn't the fact of having killed the men, and women and children too, that twisted his stomach, but the knowledge that the killings had been an offering, a deliberate mass human sacrifice.

And he suspected that when Odysseus had afterward performed the blood-brother ritual with him in the vast cave high up on Mount Parnassus, in which Trelawny had cut a gash in his own forearm with the knife made of lightweight gray metal, that had been a human sacrifice too. A *humanity* sacrifice, at any rate.

••

With an abrupt chilling shock he realized that the wind at his back shouldn't be warm, nor smell of jasmine. Quickly he reached across to take the slack reins of Tersitza's horse, but he had no sooner grabbed the swinging leather strap than a cracking sound to his left made him look back over his shoulder –

– the sound had been like a rock splitting, and for an instant he had been afraid that he would see again, here, the black bird-headed thing, apparently made of stone, that had been haunting his dreams and had seemed in them to be the spirit of the mountain –

– but it was a girl that he saw, pacing him on a third horse; and her horse's hooves made no sound on the flinty riverbed. Her luminous eyes were as empty of human emotion as a snake's, though by no means empty of emotion.

But he recognized her – she could be no one else than Zela, the Arabian princess who had died while pregnant with his child thirteen years ago. Her narrow little body was draped in pale veils that were white in the moonlight, but he was certain that they were actually yellow, the Arab color of mourning.

The smell of jasmine had intensified and become something else, something like the inorganically sweet smell of sheared metal.

She smiled at him, baring white teeth, and her soft voice cut through the clatter of the wind in the olive branches:

"Out of this wood do not desire to go,
Thou shalt remain here whether thou wilt or no."

His face went cold when he abruptly remembered that Zela had never existed outside his stories.

Even as he called, "Tersitza!" and goaded his own horse forward and pulled on the reins of hers, he recognized the lines the phantom girl had quoted – they were from *A Midsummer Night's Dream,* and it was on this upcoming midsummer's eve that he was to be consecrated to the mountain.

Tersitza was still slumped in her saddle, and Trelawny pulled his mount closer to hers and then leaned across and with a grunt of effort lifted her right out of the saddle and sat her limp form on his thighs as her cape came loose and blew away. Glancing down at her in the moment before he kicked his horse into a gallop, he saw that her eyes were closed, and he was profoundly reassured to feel for a moment her warm breath on his hand.

With one arm around her shoulders he leaned forward as far as he could over the horse's flexing neck and squinted ahead to see any low branches he might be bearing down on. Tersitza's riderless horse was falling behind, and the hoofbeats of Trelawny's were a rapid drumming in the windy gorge.

Peripherally he could see that Zela was rushing forward right beside him, a yard away to his left, though her horse's legs were moving no faster than before, and the moonlight was luminously steady on her even as it rushed past in patches all around her, and her voice was still clear in his ears:

"I am a spirit of no common rate.
The summer soon will tend upon my state,
And I do love thee. Therefore stay with me."

Trelawny didn't spare her a glance, but from the corner of his eye he could see that her veils were not being tossed in the headwind. His breath was choppy and shallow, and the wind was cold now on his sweating face.

The village of Tithorea couldn't be more than five miles ahead of them now, and this phantom didn't appear to be a physical body. As long as his horse didn't stumble in the moonlight –

Abruptly the Zela phantom was gone, but after a moment of unreasoning relief Trelawny cursed and pulled back on the reins, for somehow they weren't in the Velitza Gorge anymore.

His horse clopped and shook to a panting halt. Trelawny could feel cold air on his bared teeth as he squinted around at the dozens or hundreds of tumbled skeletons that webbed the sides of the path now, below the rocky slopes; many of the further ones straddled the bigger skeletons of fallen horses, and the bony hands of those closer clutched ropes tied around the skulls of camels on the rocky ground. The jagged moonlit ridges far above seemed as remote as the stars they eclipsed, and faintly on the wind he could hear high feminine voices combining in alien harmonies.

He made himself breathe deeply and unclench his fists from the reins and stretch his fingers. He recognized the place, at least – the devils of Parnassus hadn't transported them to some hellish valley on the moon.

They were in the Dervenakia Pass, where the army of the Turkish general Dramali Pasha had been trapped and massacred by the wild mountain Greek tribes nearly two years ago. The smell of decay was only a frail taint now on the night wind.

But the Dervenakia Pass was in the Morea – across the Gulf of Corinth, easily fifty miles south of where Trelawny and Tersitza had been a moment ago.

Very well, he thought stoutly, nodding as he forced down his panic – very well, I know the way to Argos from here, we can –

A clanking of stones on the road ahead jerked his head in that direction, and his tenuous hope flickered out.

A tall spidery thing like a black animated gargoyle stood in the moon-lit path now, a hundred feet ahead. More rocks were breaking away from the walls of the pass and tumbling across the ground to attach themselves to it, adding to its height as he watched. Its stone beak swung heavily back and forth in the moonlight.

Its lengthening black shadow shifted across the scattered white rib-cages and skulls behind it, and the high faraway voices were singing louder now, spiralling up toward a crescendo beyond the range of human hearing.

Trelawny's eyes were wide, and he wasn't breathing, or even thinking. His horse was rigidly still.

The figure ahead of them was even taller when it straightened some-what, its long, mismatched stalactite arms lifting toward the horse and riders – and though it only roughly resembled a human body, Trelawny was certain that it was female. And when it spoke, in an echoing voice like rushing water choked and sluiced and spilled by a slow millwheel –

"And I will purge thy mortal grossness so
That thou shalt like an airy spirit go,"

– he knew it was the same creature that had seemed to be riding at his left hand in the Velitza Gorge.

His face and palms tingled in the cold wind, as if damp with some moisture more volatile than sweat. *Thy mortal grossness.*

The thing ahead of them was hideous, but that wasn't why Trelawny ached uselessly to tear his eyes from it – the stones it was animating were crude, but they weren't *it*. The entity confronting him was an immortal ethereal thing, "an airy spirit" that only touched matter as a well-shod man might carelessly leave bootprints in mud, while Trelawny and Tersitza *consisted* of matter – fluids and veined organic sacs and tangled hairs, pulsing and *temporary*.

Trelawny yearned to hide from the thing's intolerable attention, but he couldn't presume to move. Abruptly he began breathing again, a harsh hot panting, and it humiliated him.

He was still holding Tersitza's limp, gently breathing little body in front of himself, as if it were an offering, and for a moment of infinite relief he felt the thing ahead shift its attention to her for a moment before fixing its psychic weight on him again.

The voice came only in his head now, again using lines from his memory but no longer bothering to cater to his fleshy ears by agitating the cold air:

I claim the ancient privilege of Athens:
As she is mine, I may dispose of her.

Since the thing had referred to Tersitza, Trelawny was able to look down at the girl. And though she was obviously as miniscule and ephemeral a thing as he now knew himself to be, her helpless vulnerability couldn't be ignored, and he scraped together the fragments of his crumpled identity enough to answer.

"No," he whispered.

The thing in the path ahead of them was growing still taller and wider, its misshapen head beginning to blot out part of the night sky, but with adamantine patience it spoke again in his head:

All the kingdoms of the world, and the glory of them.

That was what Satan had offered Christ, in the gospel of Matthew. Edward Trelawny realized that this vast thing was offering him a chance to become something like its peer, to purge him of his bodybound mortality.

How I would have soared above Byron here, he thought.

But he wrapped his awkwardly jointed arms around Tersitza and pulled her bony form to himself.

"No," he said again, and his voice was clearer now.

He looked up from under his eyebrows, blinking away the stinging sweat – and then clenched his eyes shut, for the thing was rushing at him, expanding in his view –

– but there was no obliterating impact. After some tense length of time he began breathing again, and the taint of old decay was gone, and what he smelled on the chilly mountain breeze now was tobacco and roasted pigeon.

He opened his eyes. Tersitza was still slumped unconscious across his lap on the saddle, but the giant stone form whose slopes began a mile in front of them was Mount Parnassus, its high shoulders hidden behind clouds in the moonlight. His horse stamped restlessly in damp leaves.

They were back in the Velitza Gorge again, as abruptly as they had been taken out of it – if indeed they *had* actually been out of it, and the spirit of the mountain had not simply manifested itself to him in a scene conjured, as its statements and first appearance had been, from Trelawny's memory and imagination.

To his right through the dark tangles of the oak branches he could see the cooking fires and the palikars' tents around the ruined Chapel of St. George.

He hugged Tersitza to him, already beginning to wish he could have accepted the stone thing's magnanimous offer.

The girl stirred at last, then sat up and glanced around.

"We're no further than this?" she whispered, shivering in his arms.

She had spoken in her native Greek, and he answered haltingly in the same language. "We were turned back." He was suddenly exhausted, and it was an effort to recall the Greek words. "We lost your horse."

"And my cape is gone." She ran her hands through her long black hair, feeling her scalp. "Was I hurt? I can't remember meeting Ghouras's soldiers!" She turned her pale little face up to him and her dark eyes looked intently into his. "Were you wounded?"

"No." For a moment he considered letting her believe that it had indeed been the palikars of Odysseus's rival who had forced them back to the mountain – but then he sighed and said, "It wasn't Ghouras who stopped us. It was – magic, enchantment." He wished he dared to tell her that he had been trying to save her from a fate literally worse than death – the opposite of death, in fact – and that it was her brother who had put her in that peril. "It was the mountain, your brother's mountain, that drove us back. Pulled us back."

"Enchantment?" She kept her voice down, but her whisper was hoarse with scorn. "Are you a coward after all? Odysseus is your blood-brother, and you are scared away from rescuing him by some...nymphs, dryads? *Fauns?"*

"You –" he whispered furiously, " – would be dead now, if I had not.

125

And *I* would be..."

"Dead as well," she said. "Turn back – I would rather be dead than have a coward for a husband."

Trelawny was mightily tempted to do as she said. I could be with Zela, he thought. Again. At last.

But he whispered, "Keep your voice down," and he waved toward the campfires at the old monastery, dimly visible through the trees. "Do you want to rouse Ghouras's men too?"

Yes, he could be with Zela – but Zela was a phantom who had never existed, and this girl, for all her maddening irrationality, was real, vulnerable flesh and blood.

You protect the ones you love. He clung to the thought. Even if they ignorantly resent you for it.

"We're not turning back," he said. Somewhere an owl whistled its low note through the trees.

"Give me a couple of pistols," Tersitza hissed, "and I'll go by myself!"

She was serious, and he found that his anger was gone. He admired courage, even – or especially – pointless courage. "On foot?" he asked with a smile. "It wasn't fauns and dryads."

For a few moments she was silent, and the wind rattled the dark branches around them. "I suppose it was a *vrykolakas,*" she said with apparent carelessness, though he felt her shudder as she spoke the word. *Vrykolakas* was the Greek term for vampire.

"It was," he said, "but one made of stone instead of flesh." He remembered the vision of Zela riding beside them. "Though it could mimic flesh."

She exhaled a wavering breath, and seemed to shrink in his arms.

He opened his mouth to say something more, but she gripped his wrist with cold fingers.

"I – have seen it," she said humbly, almost too softly for him to hear. "It *was* the mountain, the ghost of the mountain. I –" She looked ahead toward the imposing silhouette of Mount Parnassus, which now blocked half the sky in front of them. "I had hoped we were escaping it tonight."

"So," said Trelawny, "had I."

He flicked the reins, and the horse started forward along the familiar track to its stable in the guardhouse at the foot of the mountain, near the path that would lead Trelawny and his wife back up to the ladders that mounted to their house in Odysseus's cave, eight hundred feet above the gorge.

••

II

June 1824

"...and fortunate is he
For whom the Muses have regard! His song
Falls from his lips contented. Though he be
Harried by grief and guilt his whole life long,
Let him but hear the Muses' servant sing
Of older beings and the gods, and then
His memory is cleared of everything
That troubled him within the world of men."
　　　　　　– Hesiod's *Theogony*,
　　　　　　　　the Ceniza-Bendiga translation,
　　　　　　　　lines 96-102

After encountering the fleeing palikars just east of Missolonghi a year ago, and learning from them that Byron had died only a few days earlier, Edward Trelawny had pressed on with his own party of palikars and reached the marshy seacoast town the next day.

Down at the end of a row of shabby wooden houses under a gray sky, the house Byron had worked and died in stood on the shore of a wide, shallow lagoon. Trelawny had been escorted upstairs by Byron's old servant Fletcher, and had found the lord's coffin laid out across two trestles in the leaden glow of narrow uncurtained windows.

Fletcher had pulled back the black pall and the white shroud, and Trelawny had scowled and pursed his lips at the evidences of an autopsy – the aristocratic face bore an expression of stoic calm, though thinned by the fever that had killed him, but the disordered gray-streaked brown hair half-concealed a crude ring cut in his scalp where physicians had removed part of his brain, and the body's torso was divided by a long incision.

When Fletcher left the room, Trelawny drew his Suliote dagger and forced himself to cut off the small toe of Byron's twisted left foot. Byron was gone, but even a relic of the man might have some value as a *rafiq*.

Byron had been a co-representative in Greece of the London Greek Committee, which had put together a Stock Exchange loan to fund the war for Greek independence, and though a big sum of cash was daily expected, all that had been provided so far in Missolonghi were several cannons. By claiming to be Byron's secretary, Trelawny prevailed on the remaining representative – an idealistic but naïve British colonel called Stanhope – to let him take away a howitzer and three three-pounders and ammunition, for the defense of eastern Attica by Odysseus Androutses. Trelawny even managed to commandeer fifty-five horses and twenty artillerymen to haul the guns across the seventy-five miles back to the Velitza Gorge and the foot of Mount Parnassus, where Odysseus's soldiers built a crane to hoist the guns and crates up to the fortified cave.

Mavre Troupa, the Black Hole, was what the Greeks called the cave, but Trelawny had been relieved to get back to its lofty security.

The climb up to its broad lip was exhilarating – the last sixty feet of the eight hundred were a sheer vertical face, negotiated by clambering up ladders made of larch branches bolted to the crumbling sandstone, and the last twenty-foot ladder had a tendency to swing like a pendulum in the wind, for it was attached only at the top so that it could be pulled up in case of a siege.

The cave itself was a fairly flat terrace two hundred feet wide, with a high arching stone ceiling; the cave floor shelved up in rocky platforms as it receded into the shadows of the mountain's heart, and the various levels were wide enough for several small stone-and-lumber houses to have been built on them – Odysseus's mother and siblings lived in several of them – and the remote tunnels were walled off as storerooms, filled with sufficient wine and oil and olives and cheese to last out the longest conceivable siege. There was even a seasonal spring in the southern corner of the enormous cave, and an English engineer had begun work on a cistern so that the citizens of the cave could have water on hand even in the summer.

Philhellenes, the Englishmen who had come to fight for Greece's freedom – mostly young, mostly inspired by Byron's old poetry and recent example – seemed to Trelawny to be underfoot throughout the country these days, and, though he was one of them himself, he felt that unlike them he had shed his old links and actually become a Greek...as dark as any, attired identically, and second-in-command to a genuine mountain king right out of Sophocles.

One of these Philhellenes was the artillery officer who had come along with him on the arduous trip to Parnassus from Missolonghi, a Scotsman in his thirties who claimed to have fought in the Spanish wars; his last name was Fenton, and he had faced the rain and the muddy labor of carting the cannons to the mountain with a kind of tireless ferocious cheer – and he frequently quoted the poetry of Robert Burns. Trelawny admired him.

Trelawny's newly acquired artillerymen stayed at the guardhouse and tents below, with the bulk of Odysseus's soldiers, but Odysseus welcomed Trelawny and Fenton when they had climbed up the final ladder to the fortified cave and stood panting on the wooden platform that projected out over the misty abyss.

Trelawny had been a little nervous about the introduction, and ready to speak up for Fenton, but Odysseus seemed almost to recognize the wiry Scotsman – not as if they had met before, but as if Odysseus was familiar with some category of men that included Fenton, and had a wry and cautious respect for its members.

The bandit-chief's eyes narrowed under his striped head-cloth as he smiled, and in the mix of Italian and Greek by which he communicated with Westerners he said, "I can see that you will be of assistance and encouragement to my dear friend Trelawny," and led him away to show him where the new guns might best be mounted on the battlements that lined the cave's rim.

Satisfied that his peculiar friends would find each other's company tolerable, and eager to get out of the glaring daylight at the front of the cave, Trelawny hurried past the groups of palikars who were clustered around the several fire-pit rings on the cave floor, and leaped up the natural stone steps to the more shadowed level where his own small wooden house had been built.

He pulled his sword and pistols free of his sash and clanked them on the table, struck a flame with his tinderbox and lit a candle, then carefully lifted out of a pocket the handkerchief that was wrapped around Byron's toe. Byron was now, in a sense, physically on Mount Parnassus, *in* the mountain, but Trelawny had no idea how he might use the toe to facilitate contact with the species with whom he and Odysseus hoped to make an alliance: the creatures referred to in the

Old Testament as the Nephelim, the giants that were "in the earth in those days."

There was no contact between that species and humanity now, but there had been, as recently as two and a half years ago; and Byron had been one of their partners before the bridge between them had been broken. Trelawny believed they left some physical trace on the bodies of their human symbiotes, and so Byron's toe might at least be a reminder to them of the lost alliance – and the Nephelim, the Greek Muses, could not now even in spirit venture far from Mount Parnassus, so Trelawny had brought it to them.

He laid the little cloth bundle on the table and flipped aside the hemmed edges. Byron's toe had turned black during the month since Trelawny had taken it in Missolonghi, and he touched it gingerly.

Over the vaguely buttery smell of the candle, Trelawny was startled to catch the scent of the Macassar oil Byron had always used on his hair.

And then Byron spoke to him.

The voice was faint, and seemed to shake out of the candle flame: "Trelawny, man! This is – a huge mistake."

Trelawny became aware that he had recoiled away from the table and banged the back of his head against one of the upright beams of the house; but he took a deep breath and walked back and leaned his hands on the table to stare into the flame.

"Will you –" he began, but the voice interrupted him.

"How did you do this? How am I returned?"

"After Shelley drowned," stammered Trelawny, glancing nervously at the narrow window that looked out on the dim upper levels of the cave, "we recovered his boat – it was rammed in the storm by an Italian vessel, a *felucca* –"

"It wasn't rammed," whispered Byron's voice, "he drowned deliberately,

133

foundered his boat and sank, to save his wife and last child." The flame quivered, as if with a sigh. "But you did retrieve his boat."

Trelawny frowned, for he was certain that their mutual friend Shelley had not committed suicide; but he let the point pass and went on.

"And," he said, "and one of his notebooks was aboard, and legible once I dried it out. I let Mary take it, but not before I cut several pages out of it. In those pages Shelley explained how a man might become immortal."

"And save Greece too," said Byron's voice, fainter but even now still capable of conveying dry mockery, "just incidentally."

"Yes," said Trelawny loudly, and then he went on in a whisper, "and save Greece. That's no…mere excuse. I'm a Greek now, more than I was ever an Englishman."

"And now you mean to be a slave." The voice was almost too faint for Trelawny to hear. "To live forever, yes, perhaps – but not your own man any longer – not a man at all, but just a…shackled traitor to your race." The flame wavered. "Is there a second candle you could light?"

Trelawny snatched another candle from a wicker basket hung on the wall and lit its wick from the flame of the first candle. Not seeing a candle-holder, he drew his dagger and cut the bottom of the candle into a wedge which he jammed between two boards of the table-top.

"Our bodies," came Byron's voice again, stronger now emanating from the two flames, "those of us who wed those things, are sacramentals of that marriage bond. And Shelley meant his carcass to be lost, or burned. He was half one of them from birth, he said, and had begun to turn to stone like them. If you could bring his poor bones here, and break away what's human from what's stone, you might undo this…*overture* of yours."

"I'm not you," said Trelawny hoarsely. "I'm not afraid of becoming a god."

"Did Shelley – in this notebook that you found – *describe* these things that might be summoned back? Do you know what the Muses *look* like now?"

Trelawny didn't answer right away, for Shelley had in fact drawn a sketch of one of his supernatural mentors, on a page Trelawny hadn't cut out and taken away; the thing was grotesque, an awkward hunch-backed, bird-beaked monster.

"The physical forms they might take," Trelawny said finally, "on one occasion or another –"

"You've got two children, daughters, haven't you?" Byron went on. "Still back in England? Shelley didn't say what sort of...*fond attentions* these things pay to families of humans they adopt? If you and your mad *klepht* call up these things, your daughters won't survive, rely on it. And then – that little girl, your warlord's sister? – she'll be their prey, and change to one of them – supposing that you care about the child. All *human* family is sacrificed –"

Boots were echoingly scuffing up the stone levels toward Trelawny's house, and he hastily pocketed Byron's toe and swatted the two candles. Both went out, though the one wedged in the table stayed upright.

Trelawny strode to the flimsy door and pulled it open. The broad silhouette of Odysseus seemed to dwarf the figure of Fenton against the distant daylight as the pair stepped up the last stone rise.

"Come down to the edge," said Odysseus in Italian; he went on in Greek, "where the guns will go."

Trelawny followed the two men down the steps to the wide flat area at the front of the cave. Four six-foot sections of the stone wall had been disassembled so that the cannons might be mounted in the gaps, and Trelawny, squinting uncomfortably in the sunlight that slanted into the front of the cave, noted that only the two notches in the center of the wall threatened the road that wound its way up the gorge.

"But why aim the other two out at the slopes?" he asked Odysseus. "The Turks are hardly likely to come blundering in among the trees."

"To everything there is a season," said Fenton with a smile, "a time to gather stones together, and a time to cast away stones." His Scottish accent was especially incongruous in this cave sacred to ancient Hellenic gods. It was apparently too great a strain on Odysseus's frail grasp of English, for he turned to Trelawny and raised his bushy black eyebrows.

Trelawny slowly translated what Fenton had said.

The *klepht* nodded. "When you are consecrated," he said to Trelawny, "we will sow the same seeds as Deucalion and Pyrrha did."

"Deucalion and Pyrrha," said Fenton, rubbing his hands together and bobbing his head as he blinked out at the gorge, "I caught that bit. The giants in the earth."

Trelawny glanced at Odysseus, but the squinting eyes in the sun-browned face told him nothing.

To Fenton, Trelawny said, carefully, "You seem to know more about our purpose than you told me at first." He shivered, for the gusts up from the gorge were chilly.

"Ah, well I had to see, didn't I," said Fenton, "that you were the lot I've been looking for, before I did any *confiding*. But your *klepht* has it right – sow our army from up here."

Trelawny let himself relax – the man's caution had been natural enough, and he was clearly an ally – and he tried to imagine thousands of kiln-fired clay pellets spraying out over the Velitza Gorge on some moonlit night, the boom and flare of the guns and then the clouds of pale stones fading as they fell away into the echoing shadows.

And then in the darkness of the forest floor the things would lose their rigidity and begin to move, and burrow through the mulch of fallen leaves into the soil, like cicadas – to emerge in man-like forms at the next full moon. And Trelawny would be the immortal gate between the two species.

He laughed, and nearly tossed the coward Byron's toe out into the windy abyss; but it might still be useful in establishing the link.

"My army," he whispered.

Fenton might have heard him. "When," he asked, "will you – ?" He stuck a thumb into his own waistcoat below his ribs and twisted it, as if mimicking turning a key.

Odysseus clearly caught his meaning. *"Uno ano,"* he said.

Trelawny nodded. One year from now, he thought, at Midsummer's Eve. But even now the sun seemed to burn his skin if he was exposed to it for more than a minute or so. During the long trek from Missolonghi he had worn his turban tucked around his face during the day – and even then he had been half-blinded by the sun-glare much of the time – but he wasn't wearing his turban now.

"We can talk later," he said, "around the fires."

The other two nodded, perhaps sympathetically, and Trelawny turned away and hurried back up the stone steps into the shadows of the cave's depths.

Back in his room with the door closed, he pulled back the baggy sleeve of his white shirt and stared at the cut in his forearm. As Odysseus had predicted, it hadn't stopped bleeding. According to Odysseus it wouldn't heal until next year's midsummer, when a more substantial cut would be made in his flesh, and a transcendent healing would follow. The bigger incision would have to be made with a new, virgin knife, but apparently Mount Parnassus had several veins of the light-weight gray metal.

Trelawny leaped when something twitched in his pocket – he was used to lice, and even took a certain anti-civilization pride in finding them in his hair, but he didn't want mice or beetles in his clothing – but then the wick of the tilted candle on the table sprang into flame again, and he realized that the agitated thing in his pocket was Byron's toe.

"'Deucalion and Pyrrha,'" came Byron's faint whisper from the flame. "'Consecrated.'"

Trelawny sat down on his narrow bed, then sagged backward across the straw-filled mattress and stared at the low ceiling beams. "Why do you care," he said. "You're dead."

"I hoped to see you," said the flame, "back in Missolonghi – before I died. I don't have many friends that I relied on, but you're one of them."

"You liked me the way you'd like a dog," said Trelawny, still blinking at the ceiling. The candle-smoke smelled of Macassar oil and cigars. "You always said I was a liar."

"I never flattered friends – not trusted friends. I never let dissimulations stand unchallenged, when I wanted honesty." The frail flame shook with what might have been a wry laugh. "I only wanted it from very few."

"I never gave you honesty," said Trelawny belligerently, and a moment later he was startled at his own admission – but, he thought, it's only a dead man I'm talking to. "My mentor, the privateer captain de Ruyters – my Arab wife, Zela – none of it was true."

"I always knew, old friend. 'Deucalion and Pyrrha,' though – and 'consecration.' What ordeal is it they're planning for you, here?"

"'Old friend.'" Trelawny closed his eyes, frowning. "Odysseus has a surgeon – he's going to put a tiny statue into my abdomen, below my ribs. A statue of a woman, in fired clay."

"'He took one of his ribs, and closed the flesh where it had been.' And you want to reverse what Yahweh did, and put the woman back." Byron's tone was light, but his faint voice wobbled.

Trelawny laughed softly. "It frightens you even *now?* Reversing history, yes. When clay is fired in a kiln, the vivifying element is removed from the air — wood can't burn, it turns into charcoal instead — and this is how all the air was, back in the days when the Nephelim flourished. For the right man, the clay can still...wake up."

Byron's voice was definitely quivering now. "The Carbonari, charcoal-burners, try to dominate their trade, because of this. They work to keep it out of hands like...yours."

"The Carbonari," said Trelawny scornfully, "the Popes, the Archbishops of Canterbury! And you too — all of you afraid of a power that might diminish your — your dim, brief flames!"

Byron's ghost had begun to say something more, but Trelawny interrupted, harshly, "And *your* flame, 'old friend,' is out."

And with that he leaped off of the bed and smacked his palm onto the candle, and the room was dark again.

For a moment he thought of Byron's question — *Shelley didn't say what sort of...*fond attentions *these things pay to families of humans they adopt?* — but then he thought, *My army,* and stepped to the door to join the others, regardless of the sunlight.

••

III

June 11, 1825

"...it is our will
That thus enchains us to permitted ill –
We might be otherwise –"
– Percy Shelley,
"Julian and Maddalo"

In the month since he and Tersitza had been turned back in their attempted midnight flight from the mountain, she had several times asked Edward Trelawny about the *vrykolakas* that had barred their escape. It seemed to him that she was morbidly fascinated by it, though she wouldn't elaborate on her claim, that night, to have seen it herself.

On this Saturday noon, though, Trelawny made his hopping and shuffling way down from his house in the high inner reaches of the cave to find her sitting at a table in the sunlight on the broad stone floor at the front of the cave and talking to Fenton about it.

And another young English Philhellene, a newly arrived friend of Fenton's named Whitcombe, was leaning on the parapet close enough to hear. He had only been staying at the cave for four days now, and Trelawny hadn't yet talked to him at any length.

A cannon barrel gleamed fiercely in the sunlight just beyond their table, and even up here, hundreds of feet above the treetops in the Velitza Gorge, the air was stiflingly hot. Fenton was bareheaded, but Tersitza was wearing a white turban with the loose ends tucked across her face.

Reluctant to venture out into the direct rays of the sun, Trelawny had hung back in the shadows, and though he could hardly focus his eyes on the figures out in the glaring light, he had heard Fenton laugh.

"In ten days your teeth will be fine," said the Scotsman now in his cacophonous Greek. "You'll be able to bite through stone."

Trelawny recalled that Tersitza had been complaining of a toothache for the last several days.

"And throats," Tersitza said lightly. "I wish I had had the courage to approach her, on those nights I glimpsed her on the mountain. She *wasn't* threatening, I now believe – just – bigger than me, in all ways. Bigger than flesh."

Whitcombe turned to look toward Tersitza and Fenton, but Fenton shifted his head to glance at him; Trelawny couldn't see Fenton's expression, but Whitcombe looked away and resumed staring out over the gorge.

Fenton turned back to face Tersitza. "It's good you didn't," he said. "You're not family quite yet."

Tersitza shifted on her chair and held up her arm so that her shawl fell back. Trelawny noticed a narrow band of white cloth above her elbow, and he thought he saw a spot of blood on it.

"Almost I am, now." She let the shawl fall forward, covering the band. "But I wish I had been awake, last month, when she stopped Edward and me from leaving her. For a while, he says, she took the form of a beautiful woman."

"No more beautiful than yourself, I'm sure," purred Fenton, "and no more immortal than you'll be, in ten days."

Whitcombe moved away to the right along the parapet, toward one of the cannons that was aimed out at the hillside of the gorge. Two rifles leaned against the low wall near him.

She'll be their prey, and change to one of them, Byron had said a year ago; *supposing that you care about the child.*

At the time, Trelawny had not cared about Tersitza. *The troubles of humans was not a concern of mine.* Now his belly was cold with the certainty that her arm had been ritually cut in the same way that his had, by the lightweight gray-metal knife. Odysseus was imprisoned in Athens – could Fenton have presided over the ceremony?

Trelawny stepped soundlessly back into the deeper shadows. Ten days from now would be Midsummer's Eve, when Trelawny was expected to undergo the consecration to the mountain. He was supposed to have had the fired-clay statue inserted into his abdomen weeks ago, and the surgeon here was increasingly suspicious of Trelawny's excuses and postponements.

Where the hell was Bacon? It was almost four months now since he had gone off to retrieve the talisman from Captain Hamilton of the frigate *Cambrian*. Hamilton was the senior British Navy officer in the Aegean Sea, and his father-in-law had reportedly acquired the talisman when Percy Shelley's ashes were buried at the Protestant Cemetery in Rome two years ago.

Trelawny recalled his meeting in February with Major Francis D'Arcy Bacon, on indefinite leave from the 19th Light Dragoons.

●●

It had been the last time Trelawny had seen Odysseus; they had ridden with a dozen of Odysseus's palikars to the abandoned ruins of Talanta, ten miles east of Parnassus, to meet with the Turk captain Omer Pasha and arrange a private three-month truce. "It is the only way in which I can save my people from being massacred," Odysseus had told Trelawny; "if Ghouras will send me no supplies for my army, I can't defend the Athenian passes, and I must find what allies I can."

Trelawny had been uneasy about making a secret peace with the Turkish enemy, and he had remembered Byron's posthumous warnings about Odysseus's purpose. But he had just nodded, as if Odysseus's explanation of the meeting with Omer Pasha was entirely satisfactory.

Rain had been thrashing down outside the ruined Greek church on the night of the meeting, and an attack from Ghouras's troops in the area seemed likely, so the horses had been brought into the church still saddled, and the mutually mistrustful Turks and Greeks kept their rifles and swords close by them as they crouched against the walls or sat around the fire on the cracked marble floor.

After Odysseus and Omer Pasha had concluded their pact, and a dinner of roasted goat had been followed by coffee and the lighting of pipes, several of Odysseus's palikars had stepped in from the rainy night escorting a couple of disheveled strangers and announced that they had captured two Franks.

One of the captives, a tall sandy-haired man of perhaps forty, looked around at the scowling crowd of Greek and Turkish soldiers in the firelight and said in English to his companion, "What a set of cut-throats! Are they Greeks or Turks?"

Trelawny sat against the cracked plaster wall not far from the fire, puffing at a clay pipe, but he knew he was indistinguishable from the rest of Odysseus's men.

"Mind what you say," the other man said quietly.

"Oh, they only want our money," the first man went on. He took off his wet hat and shook rainwater onto the floor. "I hope they'll give us something to eat before they cut our throats – I'm famished."

In halting but comprehensible Greek, the man explained to Odysseus that he and his companion were neutral travelers simply out to see the country, and though neither Odysseus nor Omer Pasha appeared to believe him, Odysseus invited him to sit down and have some of the no-longer-hot goat meat.

The tall man, who introduced himself as Major Bacon, sat down beside Trelawny; and as he gnawed at a rib he stared at Trelawny.

After a while he muttered quietly, *"You've* got the Neffy brand, then, haven't you?"

"'Neffy,'" repeated Trelawny, also speaking quietly. "As in Nephelim? The 'giants that were in the earth in those days,' in the sixth chapter of Genesis?"

Bacon had dropped the goat bone he'd been holding, and now asked Odysseus for *raki,* the local brandy. Odysseus spoke to one of his palikars, and the man stood up and handed Bacon a cup of wine.

"If they're robbers," Bacon called to his unhappy companion on the other side of the fire, "they're good fellows, and I drink success to their next foray."

Lowering his voice, he said to Trelawny, "You're English? You certainly don't look it. No, I said you're a…hefty man." He forced a laugh. "But hardly a giant."

"It's all right," Trelawny told him, staring into the pile of burning logs on the ruined marble floor. "I do have the, the 'Neffy' brand, I know." He touched his forearm, but he knew that the mark showed in his face too, in his eyes.

Ah." The major retrieved his goat bone and stared at it thoughtfully. "Not…altogether happy about it, are we?"

Trelawny glanced at Bacon, wondering what this stranger might know about the ancient race that slept unquietly in Mount Parnassus, and their imminent awakening.

"Not altogether," he ventured.

"Would you…get away, if you could?"

Trelawny thought of young Tersitza, asleep in his bed back in the cave on the mountain, and sighed. "Yes."

Bacon pursed his lips and seemed to come to a decision. "Think of an excuse for you and I to talk away from these men."

After a pause, Trelawny nodded, then got up and crossed to where Odysseus sat, and whispered to him that Bacon was willing to carry a letter to the British Navy asking for Odysseus's safe passage to Corfu or Cephalonia in the Ionian Sea. With Ghouras in charge of Athens now and already trying to arrest Odysseus, it would in fact be a valuable option to have.

But ever since the day he had talked to Byron's ghost, Trelawny had been trying to figure out a way to get a message to Captain Hamilton of the HMS *Cambrian*.

"Good," said the *klepht*. "Have him write it."

Trelawny straightened, nodded to Bacon, and then led the way to a doorless confessional in the shadows away from the fire.

When Major Bacon had joined him, carrying his cup of wine, Trelawny told him about the proposed letter.

"Very good," said Bacon, settling onto the priest's bench in the confessional's center booth. "I can write such a letter, in fact."

"I do want you to write to this Captain Hamilton," said Trelawny. There was only a leather-covered kneeler in his booth, in which parishioners had once knelt to confess their sins, so he leaned against the plaster wall. "I have another purpose."

"You can tell me what to write. But – you're marked with the metal from fossile alum! And I gather you have some idea of what sort of… antediluvian creature you're a vassal to."

"Not just any vassal." Trelawny smiled unhappily and quoted Louis XV. *"Après moi le déluge."* Who are you? How do you know about these things?"

The older man grinned, though not happily.

"I was a vassal to them myself, boy, until two and a half years ago, when the link between the two species was broken in Venice. Before it was broken, I watched my wife and my infant son die, and – and met them again later, when they had crawled back up out of their graves." His voice was flat, not inviting comment on events that he had clearly come to some sort of costly terms with. "None of it troubled me at the time. I was…married, to one of the Nephelim, and the troubles of humans was not a concern of mine."

"But it – is, now," Trelawny hazarded cautiously.

"There are other wives and sons," Bacon said, "besides mine. I make what amends I can, for the sake of my soul. When I learned that some fugitive members of the Hapsburg royalty were in Moscow, hoping to interest Czar Alexander in reviving the Nephelim connection, I went there, and – prevented it. Then I learned that a Greek warlord had taken possession of the Muses' very mountain and had lately performed human sacrifices in the villages of Euboaea, so I came here." He looked at Trelawny curiously. "The warlord had a partner in those sacrifices, a foreigner."

Trelawny looked back toward the fire. "Already," he said hoarsely, "the troubles of humans was not a concern of mine."

"But it is now?"

"I didn't know – quite how jealous these things are – until an old friend told me. I have two daughters back in England, and, lately, a wife."

"Stay in touch with your old friend," advised Bacon. "We tend to need reminding."

"He's dead. He was dead when he told me."

Bacon laughed. "I'm dead myself, in *every* important respect." He nodded toward the men around the fire. "My traveling companion is one of the Philhellene rabble, whom I hired as a guide in Smyrna. He still fears death."

Trelawny wasn't sure if he himself did or not. "Listen," he said, "you've got to convince Captain Hamilton of the facts you and I know, and then have him get from his father-in-law a…piece of bone that he once stole as a souvenir."

"Ah?"

"When I got to Rome in April of '23, I supervised the re-burying of Percy Shelley's ashes. You've heard of Shelley?"

"Atheist poet?"

Trelawny frowned. "Among other things. He…apparently!…killed himself to save his own wife and son from these things. He was *born* into the family of these creatures, and even before his death he had begun to petrify. I was at his cremation in Viareggio in August of '22, and when we scraped his ashes into a wooden box, I noticed that his jawbone had not burned. But when I arrived in Rome I found that his ashes had been buried in an anonymous corner of the cemetery, and I insisted that the box be dug up again and re-buried in a more prominent spot – and I looked in the box before I buried it."

"The jawbone was gone?"

Trelawny nodded. "I questioned everyone, and eventually learned that Captain Hamilton's father-in-law had been present, and had been seen to take something out of the box, as a, a *souvenir*. My dead friend said that if I could break one of Shelley's bones right in Mount Parnassus itself, and sever the Nephelim element from the human element, that might, I don't know, constitute a *rupture* or *defilement* of the arrangement I've made with them."

Bacon shook his head. "I know the *Cambrian* is in the Aegean Sea somewhere," he said, "but it'd be God's own chore to find him and then try to get this bone, just — I'm sorry! — to save one man's family."

"I'm not 'just one man,'" said Trelawny, and to his alarm he felt the old pride welling up in him; "I'm to be the bridge," he went on quickly, "they're going to implant a fired-clay statue into my ribs, and then at this Midsummer's Eve I'll be consecrated as the overlap, the gate between the species! *I'll* be — don't you see? — the restoration of the link."

For several seconds Bacon was silent in his booth. "No," he said finally with a smile that made his gleaming face look haggard in the firelight, "I won't gain anything by killing you, will I? You *klepht* will only find another racial traitor to do it with. No lack of candidates, I imagine." He stared toward the fire. "I wonder if killing your bandit-chief would effectively prevent it."

"His one-time ally and now chief rival, Ghouras of Athens, would step in. Already he's trying to."

"And others behind him, I suppose. The Greeks can't forget Deucalion and Pyrrha or the Muses in Parnassus." He sighed and stood up. "Write your letter, I'll take it — and I'll return with this atheist's jawbone as quickly as I'm able."

Trelawny stepped away from the wall. "Before Midsummer's Eve," he said, suppressing a shiver that might have been fear or shameful hope, "or you may as well give it back to Hamilton's father-in-law to use as a paperweight."

••

Standing in the shadows near the cave's glaringly sunlit edge now, the words Fenton had spoken a moment ago rang in Trelawny's head:

No more beautiful than yourself, I'm sure, and no more immortal than you'll be, in ten days.

"Tersitza," Trelawny said loudly, stepping forward, "you and I must leave here, at once. I believe Ghouras will listen to an offer of ransom for your brother."

Tersitza's covered face turned to him, and her eyes told him nothing. "My brother knows that Ghouras will kill him," she said. "He knew it when he surrendered to him. He'll come back to us afterward – stronger."

"And you've got a spot of *surgery* to undergo, haven't you?" added Fenton cheerfully, pushing his chair back across the uneven stone floor and standing up. "Time's short."

Behind him, the newcomer Whitcombe was staring in evident alarm at the three people by the table. The wind from below tossed his blond hair.

"Do it today," said Tersitza. "You need time to heal from it. You don't want to be carried down the mountain to Delphi on a stretcher, on Midsummer's Eve!"

"I'll have the surgery tomorrow, or the day after," said Trelawny, wishing he didn't have to blink tears out of his eyes in the glare. "Today you and I ride to Tithorea."

"But Ghouras's men have blockaded the gorge," said Tersitza patiently. "Wait, and we'll be able to ride right over them." She laughed. *"Fly* right over them."

"You're not getting cold feet, are you, old man?" said Fenton. "Not the pirate prince of the Indian Ocean?"

"I keep my word," said Trelawny stiffly. I did vow at our wedding to protect her, he told himself. That takes precedence, even if she doesn't want protection.

"But – are you serious?"

"Completely."

"Ghouras will just arrest you both and lock you up with her brother."

"Ghouras wants this cave, he wants the mountain, not us – and he knows he can't take it by force. He'll negotiate." This is good, he thought – it almost makes sense.

"And you think it will help to take Tersitza with you."

Trelawny could think of no plausible reason for that condition, so he only said, "Yes."

Fenton frowned and shrugged. "Odysseus told us that you're in command here while he's away. If you're confident you can come back, and if you *want* to be carried to Delphi with a bleeding incision…"

"I heal fast," said Trelawny. He turned to Tersitza and said, "We can meet with Ghouras at Tithorea, I'm certain. We'll be back here in two days at most."

And I hope I'm wrong, he thought. I hope Ghouras's men *do* simply arrest us, and forcibly take us to Athens, away from this monstrous mountain.

Tersitza's eyes were shadowed by her turban, and Trelawny couldn't tell whether she was looking at him or at Fenton.

But after a pause her shoulders slumped and she sighed, fluttering the cloth over her face. "Very well, my husband."

"I *would* advise keeping your pistols handy," Fenton said.

"Yes of course," said Trelawny.

"Why not at least get in a bit of target practice, then?" Fenton said. "Just while the palikars climb down to get your horses saddled? Whitcombe here can join us." He peered with apparent sympathy at Trelawny. "Though I must say you look a little shaky to compete this afternoon."

"Even with a pistol I'm a better shot than you two with your carbines," Trelawny muttered, "any day."

Relieved that they had given in to his proposal so easily, Trelawny quickly called for the Italian servant he always addressed as Everett, and told him to set up a plank for a target at the far left side of the terrace.

Both Fenton and Whitcombe had rifles ready and leaning against the parapet, and now they picked them up and checked the flints and the powder in the pans.

Trelawny drew a pistol from his sash and stepped between them and the target to shoot first. When Everett had set up the board and hurried back into the shadows, Trelawny swung his arm up and fired, and though the smoke stung his already watering eyes and the boom of the shot set his ears ringing, he heard the plank clatter forward onto the stone.

He stepped forward to prop the board up again, but paused when he heard Tersitza shout urgently to one of the Greeks, "Fire the cannons!"

Trelawny knew the cannons were aimed out over the gorge, loaded with the fired-clay pellets that were to come alive at the next full moon – but it wouldn't work *now*, the statue hadn't been implanted in him yet.

He opened his mouth to ask her why –

And a sudden hard blow to his back and jaw sent him staggering forward as a rifle-shot cracked behind him; he caught his balance and straightened, dizzy and stunned and choking on hot blood, and then he coughed and spat blood down the front of his shirt and cried hoarsely, "I've been shot!"

Dimly he was aware that Fenton had rushed up and was supporting him now, shouting something, but Trelawny turned to Tersitza, who was waving at someone behind him; and a moment later the stone floor shook under Trelawny's feet as the unmistakable boom of a cannon shot jarred the terrace.

Fenton was shouting, "He's good on his own for another minute, at least! It'll take! He's –" The man's voice choked off then in a gasp, and Trelawny blinked tears out of his eyes to see Tersitza.

She was pointing a pistol of her own at him, or at Fenton.

"Not *me,* not *yet!*" Fenton screamed, and then he wrenched Trelawny around by the shoulder and spoke directly into his face: "She's pregnant, she's carrying your still-human –"

Tersitza's shot struck Fenton squarely in the chest, and he pitched over backward and rolled onto his face, his head against the base of the parapet.

Trelawny abruptly sat down on the stone floor and bent forward to let the blood run out of his mouth, and two teeth and an object like half of a big pearl tumbled out past his lips to clink in the widening red puddle on the stone. But his sight was dimming and he remotely realized that he wasn't breathing, and his ribs and skull seemed to be shattered and held together only by the confinement of his skin.

As if from far away in a ringing distance, he heard the other three cannons being fired in rapid succession.

••

The clay pellets flew tumbling through the hot air, still moving out away from the cave terrace but already beginning to fall toward the treetops and the Kakoreme riverbed. Trelawny was leaping with them out over the world, though at the same time he was still sitting hunched forward on the stone floor of the cave terrace on the mountain.

His right arm was numb and useless, but with his left hand he picked up the half-pearl and rubbed away its coating of bright red blood. Now he could see that it was half of a ceramic ball, with half of a tiny grimacing face imprinted on it.

He laid it back down in the puddle and moved his hand away.

Someone was kneeling beside him, and when he squinted he saw that it was Zela, the Arab princess whose marriage to him had been cut short by her youthful death – in his stories.

"Swallow it," Zela said. "I – can't force you!" Trelawny thought blurrily that she seemed surprised to realize that she couldn't.

••

Trelawny's consciousness had expanded as far as the mouth of the gorge to the east, and north to the three standing pillars on the round stone dais at the Oracle of Delphi, but he bent his attention downward over Mount Parnassus to look at the figures on the terrace of Odysseus's cave.

He saw the sitting figure that was himself; two holes in the back of his white shirt, to the right of his spine, showed where the rifle balls had struck him.

A figure that must have been young Whitcombe had snatched off its turban and tied one end of it to the crane boom at the edge, and was rapidly climbing down it toward the highest of the moored ladders on the cliff-face below.

The woman who was either Tersitza or Zela was speaking, and the hovering spirit of Trelawny discovered that he could hear what she said:

"Swallow it." There was urgency in her voice. "You've only got half of the statue inside you now. Swallow it and it will reform itself, and reform you. I *can't* force you! You're dying, Edward, my love – you'll *die* here, now, if you don't do what I say. Or you can be healed, and live forever with us."

He was able, too, to look in another, entirely unsuspected direction, and there he saw the Trelawny figure step toward the fallen target-plank, as behind him Fenton aimed a rifle at his back and pulled the trigger – but the gun didn't fire; Fenton gestured at Whitcombe, who raised his own rifle and fired it at Trelawny's back, and two balls flew from the muzzle in slow motion across the terrace and struck Trelawny just to the right of his spine. From this vantage point, the hovering Trelawny spirit could even see the balls – one silver, one ceramic – punch through his flesh; the ceramic one split as it glanced off his shoulder-blade and broke his collar bone, one half of the ball tearing up through his neck muscles to break his jaw and lodge in his mouth.

This was the recent past. Trelawny looked in the other new direction, but could see nothing in the future. Did that mean he would very shortly die?

You'll die here, now, if you don't do what I say. Or you can be healed, and live forever with us.

The direction which was the future must be blank because he had not yet chosen.

The Trelawny figure's shocked lungs were at last able to take a spluttering breath.

The air smelled of tobacco, sweat, and the Indian rum known as arrack.

••

Trelawny was sitting at a table in a lamp-lit Bombay tavern he remembered well, and it was an effort of his unbodied will to remember too that the place had never actually existed. In a few seconds he was able to hear noises, and then he either noticed or it became the case that the low-ceilinged room was crowded. Slaves carrying trays threaded their way between tables full of young British midshipmen in blue jackets, but Trelawny stared at the man sitting across the table from him – he was perhaps thirty years old, with black hair pulled back from his high tanned forehead, and he puffed tobacco smoke from the hose of a hookah. Unlike anyone else in the place, he had a cup of steaming coffee in front of him.

The man pressed his lips together in a way Trelawny remembered well – it used to indicate impatience at an unexpected obstacle.

"You died," Trelawny said to him carefully, "off the Barbary Coast, in a fight with an English frigate." He realized that he *could* speak, and that his wounds were gone, and that he could flex both arms. He took a deep effortless breath, wondering if it might be his last, but forced himself to go on: "And in fact you never existed at all outside my imagination." For this man at the table with him was the privateer de Ruyters, who in Trelawny's stories had taken him in as a raw, wild sixteen-year-old deserter and taught him discipline and self-control.

"If you like," said de Ruyters with a tight smile. "At that rate, of course, you're about to bleed to death on Mount Parnassus, and your Tersitza will be a widow. And you and I will never have – oh, where do I start? We'll never have stormed St. Sebastian, and saved your bride Zela from the Madagascar pirates. Zela, in fact, will never have existed." His smile was gone. "Perhaps you've forgotten her already."

Trelawny had not. He remembered, as if it had actually occurred, his first meeting with Zela: when de Ruyters's French and Arab crew had routed the slave traders of St. Sebastian before dawn and burst into the slave-huts, where Trelawny had been only moments too late to save Zela's bound father from being stabbed by one of the pirate women.

Trelawny had killed the woman and freed the dying old Arab, who as he took his last breaths had drawn a ring from his own finger and put it on Trelawny's, and had joined Trelawny's hand with his young daughter's, and had then spoken a blessing and died.

The Arab's daughter had been Zela.

Later Trelawny had learned that this had constituted a betrothal, and he had devoted the next several weeks to the strictly chaperoned courtship that Arab tradition required; when at last he had been permitted to hold Zela's hand and meet her unveiled eyes, he had known that this was, as he had put it to himself, the first link of a diamond chain that would bind him to her forever.

"She," said Trelawny, "died too. After not having ever existed either."

After? he thought, impatient with himself.

"We *can* exist," said de Ruyters irritably. "We *do,* in some branches of reality. Would you not rather have the adventurous life you had with us, than what – if you insist! – you actually had? – an undistinguished Naval career and a shabby marriage and divorce?"

De Ruyters reached across the table and gripped Trelawny's shoulder, and a confident comradely smile deepened the lines in his cheeks.

"Look, man," he said softly, waving around at the crowded tavern – which abruptly faded away, revealing a landscape that was deeper and clearer than anything Earth could provide: a remote horizon of green-sloped mountains lit by slanting amber light, crowned with castles whose towers cleaved the coral clouds; wide bays glittering in the sunset glow, stippled with the painted sails of splendid ships; parrots like flaming pinwheels shouting among the leafy boughs closer at hand. Faintly on the cool sea breeze Trelawny caught the lilt of festive music.

He couldn't see de Ruyters, but a girl stood beside him now on this grassy meadow, her slim brown body visible under her blowing yellow veils, and he knew that she would be young forever. "All these things will I give you," she told him, "if you will worship me."

Trelawny knew that it was the spirit of the mountain that was speaking to him and had been speaking to him.

"You need not surely die," the girl said earnestly. "When you swallow the stone, then your eyes shall be opened, and you shall be a god among gods, knowing neither good nor evil."

And Trelawny remembered what this same creature had said to him a month ago, when he had tried to escape with Tersitza from Parnassus:

And I will purge thy mortal grossness so
That thou shalt like an airy spirit go…

For a moment he glimpsed again the pale, sweating, tortured figure sitting on the terrace-edge of the Parnassus cave, a string of blood dangling from its mouth to the spreading puddle of blood in which lay several teeth…and the half-sphere stone.

One image or the other would have to be erased – the bright sensual immortality or the suffering organic thing in the cave. The one was imaginary and the other was real, but what hold had real things ever had on him?

A god among gods, Trelawny thought dizzily, "king of kings," as Shelley had written – "look on my works, ye mighty, and despair."

But the thought of Shelley's poetry brought back Byron's words about him: *he drowned deliberately, foundered his boat and sank, to save his wife and last child.*

Trelawny had been proud to call Shelley his friend.

The young girl still stood beside him on the green slope, near enough to touch, but Trelawny made himself look away from her. "Tersitza," he said, bracing himself and almost apologetic, "is pregnant with my child."

Then, abruptly, he was in the reeking Bombay tavern again, and in the dim lamplight de Ruyters was staring at him across the table. "Zela was pregnant too. Is."

Somewhere beyond this hallucination, Trelawny felt the cannon-propelled clay pellets clatter down onto the dirt and pebbles of the Velitza Gorge, bounding and skittering until they came to rest. They would germinate if the link between humanity and the Nephelim was established – if he swallowed the broken-off half of the little stone statue so that it could be whole inside him.

If I do it, he thought, Tersitza, with the wound of the gray metal knife in her arm, will change to one of them...and so will my child... supposing that I care about them.

Hating himself for his cowardice, Trelawny closed his eyes and reached out again with his left hand, brushed at the puddled stone surface that it encountered until his fingers closed around the split stone sphere, and again picked it up.

Torn nerves made a bright razory pain in his ribs, his neck, his jaw. He opened his eyes and saw Tersitza staring anxiously at him.

"Be healed," she said.

And he flung the stone out sideways, into the abyss.

"No," he grated to Tersitza and the mountain.

••

IV

August 1825

"For the first twenty days after being wounded, I remained in the same place and posture, sitting and leaning against the rock, determined to leave everything to nature. I did not change or remove any portion of my dress, nor use any extra covering. I would not be bandaged, plastered, poulticed, or even washed; nor would I move or allow anyone to look at my wound. I was kept alive by yolks of eggs and water for twenty days. It was forty days before there was any sensible diminution of pain; I then submitted to have my body sponged with spirit and water, and my dress partly changed. I was reduced in weight from thirteen stone to less than ten, and looked like a galvanized mummy."

– Edward John Trelawny,
Records of Shelley, Byron and the Author

It was nearly two months later that Major Bacon came at last to the cave, climbing barefoot up the ladders in the noonday sun because the height was too unnerving for him to attempt the ascent in boots. At the top of the second ladder, hanging over a drop of more than seven hundred feet, he had to shout several times to the suspicious faces that peered down at him from the parapet twenty feet above.

"Trelawny!" he yelled up at them. "I'm looking for *Edward Trelawny,* you ignorant brigands!"

You clods, you stones, you worse than senseless things, he thought worriedly. Midsummer's Eve was more than a month past, and though Shelley's charred jawbone was wrapped in an altar cloth in Bacon's haversack, it would be of no use if Trelawny had already been transformed into the new link between humanity and the Nephelim. He hoped poor idiot Whitcombe had been able to accomplish something.

Bacon allowed himself a moment to stare at the pitted limestone directly in front of his rung-clutching hands – looking up was even more terrifying than looking down past his feet at the distant rocky gorge, and he felt as if his bowels had turned to ice water. But at a scuffling sound from above he looked up again.

A girl's face had appeared now at the cave's rim, scowling down at him. "Bacon?" she called.

His stomach was too fluttery on this windy, vertiginous perch for him to do more than scream back the Greek word for assent, *"Neh!"*

The girl disappeared, and after sixty fast, shallow breaths Bacon had begun considering the ordeal of feeling for the next rung down with his bare right foot, and then putting his full weight on that rung and doing it again, back down forty feet of rickety ladders to the narrow ledge that was still seven hundred vertical feet above the roofs of the barracks and stables at the foot of the mountain…but then he heard a clattering from above and saw that several men were angling another ladder out from the cave and lashing its top end to a boom that projected out over the low wall at the edge.

Bacon had to duck when the ladder swung free, and the bottom end of it swished through the air a foot over his head.

He stayed crouched at the top of the second ladder until the third one had largely stopped swinging. It stood out at right angles from the cliff-face, and the high-altitude breeze chilled Bacon's sweating face as he reached up with one hand and gripped the bottom rung. A moment later his other hand had clutched it too, and he climbed up it rapidly, before it could swing away from the fixed ladder and leave his feet flailing free.

No more than a minute later he was sitting on the cave floor several yards back from the edge, panting and pressing his palms against the solid stone.

Five or six disreputable Greeks with rifles stood around him in the shade of the cave's roof, but their scowls might have been habitual, for the rifles were pointed at the floor.

"Trelawny?" said the girl who had peered at him over the edge. She was standing beside Bacon, dressed in a loose white chiton that left her arms bare to the shoulders, and she seemed very young. The big dark eyes in her thin face stared intently at him.

Bacon stared back, and did not see the feverish hunger he remembered seeing in the eyes of his unnaturally resurrected wife and son.

After a pause, *"Neh,"* Bacon said again. "Here?"

She nodded, perhaps just at the affirmative, and rocked her head toward the back of the cave, and then began walking up the shelved layers of stone into the deeper shadows.

Bacon sighed mightily and got to his feet.

Several little houses had been built of wood and stone on the higher levels, and the girl led him to one of them and pulled open the flimsy door.

The room within, lit by a lantern on the table, smelled like an ill-kept dog kennel, and at first the frail figure on the bed did seem to show the sick, predatory alertness of those favored by the Nephelim – but a second glance convinced Bacon that it was only extreme physical illness that gave the sunken eyes their glittering semblance of eagerness.

A dirty cloth was visible under the bearded jaw, bound over the top of the head, and the figure apparently couldn't speak; but when its eyes lit in recognition and a skeletal hand wobbled toward him, Bacon recognized the man.

"My God," he said. "Trelawny?"

The man on the bed looked toward Tersitza and touched his jaw. The girl crossed to him and worked with both hands at the knotted cloth, and when it fell away, Trelawny opened his mouth and said, clearly, "Yes."

Bacon leaned against the wall and ventured to smile. Clearly Trelawny had somehow not been granted the near-godhood that had been planned for him.

"Here I am," Bacon said, "come to redeem my pledge of rendering you a service –" He paused to look around the room. " – and to enable you to quit Greece."

"You," said Trelawny hoarsely, "are a friend indeed."

Bacon unslung the haversack from his shoulder and crouched to unstrap it. He lifted out the altar-cloth and unfolded it, exposing the arch of dark bone with its row of knobby teeth.

Tersitza was looking on anxiously, and a couple of bearded faces were peering in through the door, but there was no comprehension in their expressions.

Half of the jawbone-section was gray stone, and the hinge-end was blackened yellow bone.

"Shall I break it?" Bacon asked.

"No," said Trelawny. "It's for me to do."

He held out his skeletal arm again, and Bacon straightened up and crossed to the bed and laid the bone in Trelawny's withered palm.

Trelawny's right arm seemed to be useless, but he gripped the bone between the fingertips and the heel of his left hand, and then the tendons stood out like cords on his trembling forearm as he squeezed the thing.

Tersitza opened her mouth and took a half-step forward, then hesitated.

The bone snapped.

The floor shook, as if the whole mountain had been massively struck.

Bacon flinched, then with hollow flippancy quoted the Book of Judges: "With the jawbone of an ass you have slain your thousands."

He noticed tears glittering on the girl's cheeks, though she made no sound.

Trelawny opened his shaking hand and two pieces fell onto the floor, the stone half separate from the organic half.

"Give me the bit that was Shelley," said Trelawny, "the human half of him."

Bacon bent down and retrieved it, and handed it to Trelawny.

By the dim lantern-light Bacon looked around at their audience, and decided he could talk safely if he spoke in rapid English.

"You aren't the link between the species," he said. "It didn't happen, obviously. Why not?"

"A young man shot me," said Trelawny, "in the back, before the appointed day. He fled directly after. My people here," he added with a nod toward the girl and the men in the doorway, "caught him and wanted to kill him, but I let him go two weeks ago."

"Ah," said Bacon. After a moment he asked, "Why'd you let him go?"

"He was – trying to *save* me, actually. When he shot me. Well, save Tersitza and my unborn child, at any rate." Trelawny clutched the fragment of Shelley's jaw. "Odysseus and his agents –" He looked toward the wall, and Bacon guessed that he was deliberately not looking at the girl, " – had arranged to insert the fired-clay statue into me by a more direct sort of surgery, since I was reluctant to have it done with a scalpel; they loaded a rifle with it."

Bacon raised his eyebrows and looked at the wasted figure on the bed – clearly Trelawny's jaw and right arm had been injured. It seemed unlikely that a shot in the back could have done all this damage.

"But Whitcombe shot you first?" he hazarded.

The girl and the men in the doorway shifted at the mention of the name.

And Trelawny was staring at him. "You – know him?"

"I *sent* him, man."

"Sent him to shoot me in the back?"

"If that was what the situation called for." Seeing Trelawny's sunken eyes fixed on him, he grinned and added, "The troubles of humans is still not a *big* concern of mine. But his shot obviously didn't kill you, quite – didn't they then shoot the statue into you?"

Trelawny was shaking, and he seemed to spit. "Did I call you a *friend,* a moment ago?"

"Yes, and I am your friend. I don't indulge my friends when hard measures are needed to save them – save their souls, if not their lives." He smiled. "I have very few friends."

"God help them."

"Rather than another, yes."

Trelawny scowled at him. "Whitcombe didn't shoot me *first* – it was him that shot the bloody statue into me."

"He *did?*" Bacon shook his head. "I don't understand. Why are you – as you are, then?"

"Your man Whitcombe loaded their rifle with a *second* ball, too –
one made of silver. And he made sure that he was the one who fired it,
so the addition wouldn't be noticed."

Bacon laughed softly. "Ah, clever boy! Silver repels vampires, certainly. And that…*cancelled* the stone one?"

"No, damn you. The stone ball, the statue, broke, as it broke my bones;
half of it broke my jaw and came out through my mouth. 'Jawbone of
an ass' there, if you like. All the *silver* ball accomplished was to restrain
them –" Now he did glance at the girl, " – from forcibly feeding it to me,
shoving it back in." He exhaled harshly. "I had to *choose* to throw away
the mountain's offer of salvation – and accept," he added, waving his
frail hand at his diminished body, "this, instead."

Bacon nodded and crossed his arms. "I learned some things about
your chum Shelley," he said, "while I was off fetching that there bit of
bone. It seems he made a costly choice too, finally, at the end – and he
didn't get the privilege of complaining about it, after."

Trelawny managed to draw himself up in the bed, and Bacon was
more able to recognize the man he had met on that rainy night in
the ruined chapel at Talanta six months ago. "I'm not complaining,"
said Trelawny. "Just giving you honesty." He closed his eyes and sighed
deeply. "I only give it to a very few."

••

Four days later at noon they left the cave – Trelawny and his Italian
servant, Bacon, Tersitza and her younger brother. Odysseus's mother
and his palikars chose to stay behind in the Muses' mountain. A rope
had to be tied under Trelawny's arms and run through the pulley on
the boom, for he couldn't negotiate the ladders.

At the foot of the mountain at last, Trelawny was lifted into a saddle, and it was all he could do to keep from falling off the horse as their party wound slowly down the dry Kakoreme riverbed. Trelawny was squinting in the sun-glare, but now only because of his long stay in the dimness of the cave.

Tersitza sat cross-legged on a mule, and she replied only in curt monosyllables to the remarks Trelawny was able to articulate. They passed the stones marking Fenton's grave without comment.

The bone fragment of Shelley's jaw was tucked into Trelawny's sash beside his pistols and his sword, and he touched the angular lump of it and wished he believed in God so he could pray.

From behind them a deep boom rolled down the gorge, followed a moment later by another, and Trelawny knew that the palikars in the cave were firing the guns as a parting salute, with no projectiles loaded. The ready tears of long convalescence blurred his vision.

In the dirt and pebbles and fallen leaves all around them, he knew, were the kilned clay pellets that had been fired from those same cannons two months ago – and he wondered now if they had quivered with newborn alertness, in the moment between their landing and his rejection of Parnassus's offered gift.

Another cannon shot boomed away between the ridges of the gorge.

For a moment as the echoes faded he was sure he caught, faintly, the high female voices he had heard singing on the night four months ago when he had tried to take Tersitza and himself away from the mountain – but they were very faint now, and he was bleakly sure that they no longer sang to him.

He thought of Odysseus, the real Odysseus of Homer, tied to the mast and intolerably hearing the song of the sirens fading away astern.

And in a vision that he knew was only for himself, he saw the great stone spirit of the mountain rise beyond the trees to his right; its vast sunlit shoulders eclipsed the southern ridges, and its dazzling face, though it was an expanse of featureless gleaming rock, somehow expressed immortal grief.

And I do love thee, it had said to him on that night. *Therefore stay with me.*

As he shifted his head the thing stayed in the center of his vision as if it were a lingering spot of sun-glare, or else his gaze helplessly followed it as it moved with voluntary power, and he found that he had painfully hitched around in the saddle to keep it in sight, until it overlapped and merged with the giant that was Mount Parnassus, receding away forever behind him.

●●●

AFTERWORD

Trelawny was certainly a liar who eventually came to believe his own melodramatic fabulations – though his last words were, "Lies, lies, lies" – but his adventures on Mount Parnassus did happen. He really was the barbaric right-hand man of the mountain warlord Odysseus Androutses, really did marry the thirteen-year-old Tersitza, and he really was shot by William Whitcombe in the high Parnassus cave, and with no medical aid simply waited out his recovery. His injuries were exactly as I describe them, and he really did spit out, along with several teeth, half of one of the two balls Whitcombe's rifle was loaded with.

He survived, and in later years asked Mary Shelley to marry him (she declined the offer), swam the Niagara River just above the falls, and in his old age was lionized in Victorian London society as the piratical friend of the legendary Byron and Shelley – and even of Keats, though in spite of the many colorful stories he would tell about his acquaintance with that poet, Trelawny had never actually met him. Trelawny died in 1881, at the age of eighty-eight, and the romantic autobiography he had constructed for himself, partly extravagant truth and partly extravagant lies, endured whole for a good eighty years after his death.

–T. P.